ALAIN BRÉMOND-TORRENT

"Darling, it's not only about sex"

Chapitre
1

[Vlam!]
Someone has let the front door slam, unintentionally, perhaps carelessly.

The bags under my eyes, they weigh like suitcases, like it is too early to wake up. I can hear Jude's slippers sliding on the floor of the warehouse below my bedroom, like skis, making a winter season type of sound right in the middle of summer. The daylight has already invaded my room, tearing yesterday's page off the calendar, switching today on with the best wishes from mother nature. Noise and light are pairing to take me out of slumber, i'm keeping my eyes closed, consciously knowing that within the spin of the planet, the night is over. I should set up some blinds on these plastic windows.

[Vlam!]
The door slammed again, without attention, probably carelessly.

   "I forgot my phone!" Chloe shouts as she comes back in.

"I'm shocked! That must be the first time this happens" Jude replies, she laughs out loud.

Chloe tends to forget things easily, like the fact that she lives with other housemates who may appreciate sleeping in on a Saturday morning.

Jude and Chloe have been going out for a while, they live in their couple bubble sharing the space with the five of us in the warehouse, i hear they're kissing goodbye. They're wishing each other a good day, sharing a short moment of tenderness as the effect of his joke is fading out. If they only knew that, just above their head, someone was having a healing dream, they would have acted perhaps more discreetly.

[Vlam!]
Chloe is gone to work and everybody knows it.

The fulfilling impression from the dream is disappearing progressively, the taste of an unexpected erotic adventure still remains. This type of vibe has been too rare in my life lately. I force myself to re-dive into it to experience the episode that was going to follow before i get totally awake, but my awareness is growing. I can feel the air on my feet as they are popping out of the sheet, i can feel the spring of my mattress bothering my right elbow.

A short moment ago, if my short memory is good, i was in a small car with a long dark haired woman, i think she was Indian, or South American, she looked similar to the girl i used to work with at the café. She was driving frantically, the vehicle was only touching the road with two wheels when taking roundabouts. She was pressing on the accelerator pedal like it was a kick drum, slaloming between cars in traffic hectically, quietly focussed and incredibly active at the same time, waving her dark eyebrows to comment events on the road. She was taking turns breathlessly, daring gravity and the car mechanics until we entered the courtyard of a council estate where she parked hurriedly with a controlled skid on the gravel. The building strangely looked similar to the one where i used to live in my childhood. Weird.

Out of the car, she rushed upstairs to her flat, chased by her long black hair. She opened the door with a dextrous wiggle on the key and turned on the ceiling fan. I followed, went in, closed the door behind me and got instantly pushed against it. She wanted kisses but her lips were trying to catch breath. I was continuously surprised, politely behaving like a guest should. Her breast was pressing against my chest, she bit my cheek and said, "Come!" then rushed to her bathroom.

She wouldn't stop running and i wasn't questioning the rush, trying to follow her at a pace that was closer to mine, "Come! Come!" she was repeating while opening the tap of the bathtub full blast. I was observing her wetting her arms, putting the rubber bath plug into the bath hole, adjusting water temperature with the sensitivity of her hands, seated on ceramic. As the steam started to form, she turned back towards me, putting her fingers in her mouth with a will in her eyes to find complicity, "It is hot enough now, try" and pointed them at my mouth.

I came closer, tipped my head to one side, unrolling my lower lip like a red carpet for her hand, i had matched some expectations she had. "Don't let the temperature drop down!" she added, blushing, tickled by the comedy of the erotic situation. She took her top off and bent her back with the grace of a ballerina to cling on the other side of the bathtub with her hands, arching like a bridge above the steam, balancing her body with her legs, letting her hair touch the water.
I leaned over her, following her lines felinely with my lips. She tilted to one side, found balance with her body to get a hand free to grab her phone out of her back pocket and with a natural flick, took a picture of us bending above water and threw it on the heap of clothes near the laundry basket.

She changed position to arch the other way, penetrating the surface of the water with the curve of her derrière to sit at the bottom of the tub. Seeing her in the water, still in her clothes, made us smile mockingly, as unconventionalism often does. I was observing her trousers getting drenched, her alluring spectacle, my eyes had too much to capture for just the two of them. She took off her red bra with a gymnastic move and raised her chest to say, "Take a picture of me!". I turned my head towards where her phone landed before hearing, "With your phone!" and so i did and shot the scene repeatedly while she was struggling to take her pair of jeans off in the narrow space of the bathtub. She was contorting her body, playing with sexy postures, and with all her charms, she slipped and got stuck in an awkward position.

We laughed at her state being tied up in her denim, asking for help. I tossed my phone near hers on a towel and stepped in warm water in my clothes, not really helping, mostly taking advantage of the situation to study her sensitivity. Her skin was soft and humid, with the tip of her breasts raising like little islands in the sea, her hair was glossily wet, drops were sliding across her face and on her lips. She was so beautiful, so desirable and full of desire, like a summer fruit begging to be bitten by exhibiting attractive colours. I was smitten, about to land my mouth on hers and amongst all sparkles, [Vlam!], the door under my bedroom slammed.

It is not so much because i am French, and i wouldn't make a big deal out of it if i had sex regularly, but it must be at least six months since the last time i slept with someone. Six months without sex is a lot, being French or not, just being human.

My libido has been decreasing progressively as my sexual activity has gone down, i didn't see it going. Not having someone in my mind or around me who inspires my desire and sensual prowess didn't help. Obviously, the less i have sex, the less i feel the need to make out with someone, or at least until the sunny days come back. Luckily, even in London, spring and summer know how to revive that thing, they tickle my senses, they even make my subconscious create erotic scenes in my slumber to remind me how vital it is to turn the engine back on, because after six months of zero real steamy entertainment, it could be a little rusty. I talk from experience, it is not the first time that this happens, once i haven't had sex during a whole year. It was in 2012. In 2012, i went through a sex desert. By the end of that year, it felt like the end of the world that some people were predicting. I remember, it was hard to believe for most of my friends, some of them were inviting me to organised dinners or drinks, discreetly introducing me to their single mates, some others even offered to sleep with me just to get me back on track. Curiously enough, i was never in the mood for mingling and it was difficult to explain. I did not try to hide the fact that i didn't feel like having sex with anyone, i was naturally in touch with my emotions, unlike the type of men from my father's generation, i was ok to talk about my feelings but still, some people couldn't take it, describing me as fussy, arrogant or even misogynist. Perhaps i wasn't expressing myself well enough, i would say that i was freed from desire, purifying my mind and senses like in Gala's song.

That year, i learned so much about relationships by not being in any. I understood that i had to improve myself before trying to get with anyone as the type of discomfort i was finding with different women became recurrent. It took me time to comprehend that it is not because situations look familiar that they are necessarily good for me and that i should change my mind to get out the loop. It could sound simple in a sentence, nonetheless quite hard to achieve. It is a real exercise to repeat every day, to analyse and re-organise myself. Some people go to the gym to get more attractive physically, i've chosen to study the past and patterns i was trapped into. It is more about dropping than lifting weight. The work has helped me a lot and even if i feel better about myself and the world today, i could only affirm that despite all thoughts and recommendations, the best remedy i found so far to deal with relationships, is to stay on my own and enjoy solitude. It is certainly not very courageous but i find the comfort that it comes with quite necessary to appreciate other aspects of life.

Some see it as selfishness or fussiness, nonetheless, it is less of a mess i guess.

Of course, not being sexually adventurous doesn't mean that i can't appreciate sensuality anymore, especially when the weather is warm and the outfits are getting more alluring, but somehow, i tend to abandon the prowl quickly. The desire often fades out to give space to creativity. When i can be freed from my other commitments, i am usually more inclined to think about ideas than ladies.

Having said that, i decided to change the game recently, to do an effort to reconnect with my sexual energy. My body needs it, probably my mind too. It is not so much about horniness, it is about awareness of my well-being. So i downloaded a couple of online dating applications on my phone to see what it is like to engage with new women without even having to get out of my room.

So far, from the ones i matched with, there is Amy who keeps me chatting. A British brunette with a cute face and a funny presentation of herself. At this stage, it is humour that makes the difference for me and she made me smile a few times with her messages. The other matches so far, look prettier than interesting and i am not so eager to push myself to meet someone i don't feel inspired to talk to. There were others who seemed attractive but they deleted me after the first sentence i wrote to them. I'm still learning how to express myself on the platform but the digital distance and the human values that i learned in my pre-smartphone education don't seem to match together very well sometimes. Anyway, Amy and myself planned to see each other tonight. It will be the first time we meet and the first time for me to go on a date with someone i never physically met before. I am not saying that i have much expectations from Amy, or from myself liking Amy, but she seems funny and humour goes well with a drink. A bit of happening will be nice, after six months without dating anyone, even having a glass with a woman sounds adventurous. I feel out of the game, out of sensual shape but i'm finally up for it.

Tonight's date has set up the intrigue for today, but this is later and for now i am trying to reconnect with my dream and with this sensual woman my subconscious generously brought to my vision as i still feel morning glory. It is impossible to experience the end of the story naturally without the interference of my conscious imagination. Her character was incredible, her reactions were totally unexpected, she was surprising me with everything she did, i wouldn't have been able to write such a scenario, i don't even like speed driving.

If i keep my eyes closed and focus on the atmosphere

i was in just a moment ago, i could perhaps transport myself back to the erotic zone. It is almost still there but i can't quite get the sensation of the water from the bath anymore nor the frenzy of excitement. It isn't the same, it's practically gone, like a melted ice cube in a drink, it has influenced the temperature though. I'm flicking through the images that remain from the dream. I'm trying to feel her wet and warm skin again. Her warm and wet skin. I'm trying ways to recapture the volatile feeling, to recreate the mirage. I would like her to get closer, i want to feel her wet breast sliding on my chest, i want to feel her body on my lips, under my fingertips, my palms, i want to be with her in the intimacy of the bath, in the secret of my bed sheet, she would be so warm inside. I am getting hornier, she is breathing louder, my touch is firmer, attentive. Her long hair, her mouth, they're all shining. I clench my hand tighter and accelerate. She is moaning in my ears, the pleasure is dominant, imminent, the itch has increased to its maximum, the convulsion is getting nearer, at fire temperature, i grab a sock on the side of my bed and end up in it.

A storm goes through me, an electro shock, tensing my muscles and relaxing every part of my body, changing everything for the better.

Socks are quite convenient to conclude masturbation. There's always one laying around my bed, their shape is well suited and i can just throw the whole thing onto my pile of laundry when i'm done as if nothing happened.

Because that is the thing with masturbation, it never officially occurs. However natural and beneficial it could be, rare are the ones who dare admitting masturbating, as if it was a shameful thing to do. Somehow, it is cool to talk about having sex with someone but it is not cool to talk about having sex alone. In a similar way, taking a selfie is uncool but it is ok to take a picture when posing with someone. I don't get why solitary acts are so looked down upon. Masturbation fixes a lot of problems by releasing stress, it is a quick answer to libido. It is a bit selfish but it definitely helps not having to display one's horniness in front of others, which can only serve elegance. In every way, masturbation is quite handy.

There is a noise of footsteps on the tiles above my head. The roof is thin enough, i can guess these are not the ones of a bird, it is definitely a cat walk, walking slowly and confidently, it must be Wally.

My bedroom must be the smallest i have ever had in London and probably the cutest. Situated just under the roof of the warehouse, in a triangular shape. It is made of such thin walls and cheap material that when it rains, i get bombarded by the sound of drops knocking, when it's windy, there is air entering through cracks in the wall, when it's cold outside, the bedroom gets colder than the temperature in the communal living space and vice versa when the weather is warm. There are no windows that open to the outside, only sliding plastic windows that let the light enter from the main space and from the glass door that leads to the roof terrace. But despite all of these features, the inspiration i get in here is quite amazing.

The warehouse used to be a textile factory before being converted into a living space. The street carries a few of these, most of them contain artists, fashion heads, musicians, photographers or geeks. It is the seven of us in here, with six bedrooms, three on each side of the warehouse, on two levels. There is a huge common space in the middle with a homemade ping pong table, a big silver square table, a multitude of plants with little trees growing up in pots towards quite a high ceiling. There are sofas here and there, an old organ, a small piano, a mini bar, there are lingering decorations from past theme parties and various other vintage objects and unusual design features. There is a fireman pole to slide down from the two top bedrooms where Lyla and Gingembre live. Those two have got the same triangular shape bedroom as mine, with an oblique ceiling following the slanted angle of the roof. I wish there was a toboggan on my side so i could go to the living space with as much ease as the girls. Instead, there is a narrow and steep wooden staircase, a bit like the ones that are on boats, which can be quite dangerous if you're not totally sober or not attentive enough to the way you conduct your way down. Harry, who lives in the bedroom next to mine, doesn't seem to be worried by the height nor the steepness too much, he has used these stairs in states where even flat ground would challenge body balance and he's always been fine with them. This staircase leads to the bedrooms and to a flat rooftop, which we use to grow plants and vegetables, it brings an extra dimension to the place, especially during a summer day like today.

This place is the place where i stayed the longest in London, and London has also become the city where i lived the longest. I don't know what makes a place the place where one belongs to, if it is where one was born, if it is where one has most of his family, if it is where one currently lives or has lived the longest, but i can say that it feels like home in this neighbourhood to me. And even if the gentrification makes the housing prices rise crazily and we're never certain that we can afford to live in the area for much longer, it really feels like home, which can be a rare experience in London.

It seems impossible to get back to sleep. I should be tired by now considering i was working quite late last night on my music. The moon must be full this weekend i reckon. I can feel it in my energy level. Usually, when i wake up that early, i tend to fall back asleep, especially after releasing sexual tension. It even becomes annoying to be lying flat, i'd bet it is full moon this weekend.

I push on my arms to reach a seated position. I grab the pillows that spent the night by my side and organise them to create a pile behind me. I lay my back against the improvised installation and try to adjust the comfort. I sit up to find the right position and lean back on the stack of feathers.

Starting the day with meditation and deep breaths

improve the journey i was told recently, i thought i should try, so i've been dipping my toes and the rest of my body in it for nearly a month. So far i find it quite difficult, as i usually find things harder in the morning, although i have done it everyday since i started. I'm forcing myself every morning to take a moment to sit, looking at it as an appetiser before breakfast that is going to make the day better. It is hard to tell what it is bringing but it seems to help me pollute a little less, to send fewer unpleasant vibes into myself and the world around me. However, i am not yet too comfortable with the lotus position, so i'm adopting a kind of a relaxed, peaceful seated posture instead, which is good enough for me to chant Ohms. Ohms have a special way to resonate in my throat, down to my rib cage into my belly. They're the window wipers that clear my mind.

"Ohm" i

Chapitre
3

Wally is walking back, i recognise the weight of his paws strolling on the roof again. Wally is the main cat of the neighbourhood, probably the strongest, he lives on the top floor of the next warehouse down the courtyard, same level as here. Wally often roams around the block, his turf, he knows the back streets, shelters, bins, staircases and window sills of the area better than anyone, he also knows the inside of most people's houses. Wally wanders everywhere regardless of whether he has permission to wander there or not. He is walking above my head, i can hear the pride in the rhythm of his stroll.

Like magic, some music appears in the air, out of nowhere, like a mirage, like the fluff in my belly button. Jude has put a vinyl to spin on the turntable, it is Philip Glass's 'Glassworks'. The intro of this record turns out to be absolutely delightful to wake up to. The melody flows and shines like a fresh stream, i'm following the current, swimming in a static position thanks to Jude's inspiration. I stay there a little longer, seated on my bed, just under the ceiling, not too far from the sky. An expanding yawn urges me to stretch my back, my legs and my arms, a little bit of wet appears on my fingers when rubbing my eyes. The yawning tears, pearls of innocence, i let them shine on my skin.

Yawning feels good, it aerates the mind. With one hand, i pull the sheet to the right like magicians do when they reveal a magic trick, but not as majestically. I bring awareness to my lower body and stand up, keeping my head down as the slanted ceiling is still too low for my height by the middle of the bedroom. The clothing rail is covered with nonchalance. I grab a pair of light fabric trousers, the Japanese type, and wrap my lower nakedness with them. I pick a light blue shirt that loiters on there too and organise it around my chest and arms, dealing with the necessary amount of buttons to close the curtain over my belly.

My guitar is on the floor in the middle of the room. Sometimes, she gets to share my bed with me, as i find it interesting to write music during quiet moments or if i pass out while following a melody, but for some reason, i left her on the floor last night, on her back with the strings up. She looks left alone although it is probably better for her not getting used to sharing my bed too often so she doesn't get jealous when a woman spends the night with me. I'm actually going on a date tonight, you never know what could happen.

The mirror on the side says there is some sleep in the

corner of my eyes and a jungle on my head. My hair has been flattened on the sides, giving a Rockabilly attitude to my face. It looks like it's been partying all night and is still having a crazy time. I work my hands through the wilderness to quickly re-organise the shape but nothing changes much so i let the party continue up there. My reflection is kind to me this morning, i smile at it and it smiles back at me.

I slip into my slippers. These slippers were not sold as slippers when i bought them, they became slippers. They were bought as moccasins from a summer collection of an Italian brand that i bought in Covent Garden a few years ago. I stopped wearing them outdoors when they started to show holes on the front, although i must have walked with them quite a few miles out there with these holes on, or just with one hole when there was only one hole. To be honest, i didn't really mind the aesthetic the holes brought to their style, people wear holes on their T-shirts, on their jeans, i didn't mind them on the shoes, and because they always became comfier, i logically kept choosing them as part of my outfit during sunny days. The only thing that is bothering me about them is when they attract my friend's jokes too much, because they look like open mouths, they get names sometimes. Of course i am aware that the lack of prestige they display is not necessarily welcomed in some circumstances, but to wear indoors or to go to the corner shop, they're fantastic. However, some friends are right, if you look at them from the front, from a cat's perspective, you may have the impression they are talking to you.

The walls around the door shake as i open it, the handle creaks, i feel like an elephant.
A glance at the communal living space, Jude seems absorbed by what's happening on his laptop, he's working already. I walk towards the roof and open the door that leads to it, in a few steps i am outside.

The sun has space for itself in the sky, little white sheep are passing by in the distance, floating with ease, carrying away their droplets of water. They look like lost tourists when most of the locals have gone on holiday.

Hopefully no one is watching in my direction from the high building across the courtyard because the way i'm currently stretching parts of my body must look quite ridiculous, but it feels good experimenting with positions, following my inspiration, it feels right pulling on these muscles, it feels better than worrying about who is watching.
There's a French expression that says 'Ridicule doesn't kill you' and there's an English one that says 'Curiosity killed the cat', i tend to balance the two out and stay alive.

Palms up, i'm stretching my back, provoking another big yawn, i'm staring at the sun until i sneeze, filling up my eyes with solar energy until my whole body reacts with a convulsion. It is shaking my brain, clearing up my lungs, i'm projecting little blobs of spittle into the air. Sneezing and yawning seem to operate without the need of my consent, awakening parts of my body i couldn't stimulate with any gymnastic position. I let my body talk, naturally, independently, like a good friend i've known for years who i trust and share the adventure of life with. It is talking to me, it is asking me to empty one part of it and fill up another. I must go back inside, i can't really take a piss on the roof and i need to drink something.

The sunrays are heavy, i could almost measure their weight on my skin disappearing as i walk back inside. Jude hasn't changed position, the record player is still throwing melodies to the living room, "Good morning" i say, as i carefully step down the staircase, "Good morning Brémond" Jude replies, keeping his eyes to the screen, the narrow stairs keep me on my toes.

There are bicycles stacked in the hallway under my bedroom and an old golden mannequin with a painted face, she is called Gala. There are two cubicles in the bathroom, one that says 'Gentlemen' on its door and another that says 'Ladies' but these signs are just for decoration, no sexism here. Having said that, i have seen polite guests waiting by the door of their gender when the other toilet was available, some people are really considerate. Some others, on the other hand, are way more loose. Once, during a party, someone broke the ceramic of the toilet, the main part, i still wonder to this day how it happened and how many people it took to get it to that state. It just can't be the result of a heavy digestion, half of the toilet was on the floor. Perhaps someone was inspired by the artistic style of the warehouse and felt like doing an avant garde installation in the cubicle, perhaps a re-interpretation of Marcel Duchamp's work, i am still not sure. The thing is, whoever did it was amongst my guests, and since the time one of the skateboarders crew jumped on the ping pong table during a party, my friends don't have the best reputation, so it didn't help to improve the image of my mates in general. Anyway, it is fixed now, there are only a few scars left on the white ladies throne.

The gentlemen's cubicle comes with a shower, the ladies one has a sink, both of them run water at different temperatures but when the hot tap of the sink is on, the shower water gets colder and it is never the other way round. The logic there seems to follow the rules of gallantry, although everyone here wouldn't mind avoiding that inequality when we're under the stream and the only accessory we're wearing is running water. I lift the toilet seat up and take advantage of being a man for not having to sit to empty my bladder.

I shake my male attribute, use a piece of the roll to absorb the last drops, re-wrap it all like a judoka and flush the toilet. It probably didn't need that volume of water to transport it all to the place it gets transported to, nonetheless it is all gone.

The bathroom sink comes with two separate taps. One says 'cold' on the top, one has 'hot'. Thanks to those it is easy to guess which one is the cold tap and which one is the hot so that is one problem solved. The difficulty here is to get water at a moderate temperature without having to take time to fill up the little sink. After all these years living in the UK, i still haven't found a convenient solution to this problem.

Life goes on, i push on the head of the hand soap bottle and get a sample from its long nose. This one is kind of fancy, Magritte must have got it from work. There are many good sides about living in a shared house of seven people, one of them is to have a Finnish housemate who brings her refined touch. The smell is calling me from the South of France, there's a mix of lavender, thyme and rosemary creating a hint of Provence in the heart of my hands. I can't hear the noise of the crickets singing the summer, nor the mosquitos eager to bother my skin but the effort is quite remarkable. This bottle delivers an impression of where i come from in a translucent liquid, just by a push on the top of its lid.

The little smoked bathroom window is slightly opened, i can hear a neighbour coughing in the courtyard, i can hear the pedals of a bicycle making an unhealthy noise too. Peeking outside, the atmosphere looks different than most days, it is warmed by the summer, this spectacle has been rare lately in this part of the world.

I tap my fingers and palms on the hanging towel and walk back to the living room finishing drying my hands on the sides of my fisherman trousers. Jude is sat down by the silver square table looking through a window from his computer. He is wearing a mustard T-shirt that matches his blond hair, i'd say the tone is more French Dijon than English Coleman. I get to one of the two fridges behind him, pull on the handle, it sounds like a giant kiss. I grab the smoothie from my shelf, unscrew the lid, raise the bottle above my head and let it downpour. Summer has invaded the open space, families of dust particles are travelling through sun's rays coming from the big square windows, fridges are humming.

"What are you up to today?" Jude mumbles.

This type of mumbled question doesn't require much of an answer. It is just a civilised acknowledgement of my presence, a bubble of kindness coming out to the surface with no big intention. I reply monosyllabically, "Work" and keep to myself the question i should send back to him, the boomerang could delay the train of thoughts Jude is currently boarding. He's been quite stressed these days with the writing process of his band's new album. It is their second and it is always a hard one to make, especially after the fair success they had with the first one. I sense it is a busy morning for him, i shall not insist, we'll connect later.

The temperature is delicious, i'm gonna have a grapefruit on the roof under the morning sun, there must be one left in my cupboard waiting to be undressed.

My cupboard is neighbour to the spice cupboard and today again someone has left a bottle of spices on my shelf instead of putting it back where it should be. It is clearly nothing but still, it provokes a reaction in me that belongs to the spectrum of irritation, and it makes me react instinctively with a French swear word, "Putain".
'Putain' literally means 'prostitute', but the meaning has evolved with the years, it has left the red light district to settle as a daily word, it is quite common, it lives near the onomatopoeias area, because, phonetically, it is such a convenient word to express when having to emphasize a feeling as it almost acts as an exclamation mark. Still, it is considered as a swear word and using it in a non-swear word environment could attract a bad look or a verbal backdraft. Saying 'Putain' helps to release adrenaline which is why people say it so often, and the polite ones would have to find a substitute to get that rush. My mother, for example, who doesn't permit uttering the word in the presence of children, would say 'purée' which means 'mashed', she would also say 'mercredi' instead of 'merde', which means "Wednesday' instead of 'shit'. The practice of that verbal gymnastic can be quite challenging because it feels so natural saying 'putain'. Today some curry powder has invaded my space, probably thinking the herbs are always greener on the other side of the cupboard, i place it back to where it belongs, i guess the bottle was curry-ous.

The grapefruit is jumping in my hand with a little help from my wrist and arm, it is spinning in the air a dozen centimetres above my fingers, obeying gravity, it makes a noise when i catch it that is almost therapeutic, two skins meeting each other in the action, i dreamt of something similar earlier.

The record is still spinning but there is no more music coming out of the speakers. I put the fruit ball on the shelf, pull the needle to one side, flip the vinyl crêpe and delicately place the needle back into the groove. I roll the grapefruit to the edge until it falls onto my hand and borrow the staircase to go back in the sunshine.

Rays of sun are falling on the terrace, landing on my feet and face, i am sitting on the big red bean bag, at roof altitude, three floors high, with my head in the sky. Friendly little sheep are migrating to the North, probably to join their family back home.

The grapefruit peel is creating a funny 'S' shape that could stand for 'sun', 'summer' or 'succulent' as i am about to take the whole skin off in one piece. The type of achievement that brings me a form of contentment akin to the one i get when throwing a crumpled piece of paper in a bin from a distance. I open the ball, tear the segments apart and peel off the inner skin to only save the thinnest flesh. It is shining in my hands, like still juicy flames, it is fire and liquid altogether, spritzing my fingers, i find it sexy.

A light breeze softly shakes my hair, i'm contemplating the neighbourhood from aloft, looking in the distance towards the South. I can see the big wheel of London eye on the other side of the river, religious and business buildings pointing to the sky in the horizon, cranes that are working on making some more.

My housemates have set up pots around the edges of this old grey platform to grow plants. There are tomatoes, courgettes, strawberries, mint, thyme, rosemary and other plants that i wouldn't know how to name. There's also a little palm tree, which is my only contribution to that garden. I brought it up here a few weeks ago without much of a plan, it just came to me. I was walking back from the Jewish bakery, it was lying on the ground in the alley, with soil hanging from its roots on one end and green leaves on the other. Someone left it there like a piece of old furniture. It didn't feel right to let it perish there so i grabbed it and carried it home, hoping on the way that it could possibly come back to life and bring to me a familiar silhouette from where i was born. Palm trees or olive trees of the French Riviera, having one of the two here on the roof touching the sky is like re-creating a link between my roots and my current life, it draws symmetry.

It is now in a pot, however, it is hard to tell if it is going to live for much longer. The few remaining leaves still show some green colour despite the growing yellow but i am wondering if the pot is big enough for it to survive. The palm tree is about a meter high and the pot is the size and the shape of a large watermelon. Perhaps the roots are too short, perhaps they need special nutriments, perhaps it needs a wetter soil. It's been raining most of the time since i brought it up here so i rarely thought of

31

watering it, but today is the third sunny day in a row we had and perhaps it is getting thirsty.

I never resurrected any major plants before, i don't know much about the greenness of my fingers. I am not sure if i can do much for it apart from sending it positive thoughts, feelings and love, sometimes these three make magic happen though. Anyway, it looks good there, better than lying down on the street, and if it is dying, then, may its last moments be surrounded with love and admiration.

It's been sunny for three days, if it rains tomorrow, someone will say summer is over.

The brick walls of Hackney, my passion for London has never ceased. These bricks sit next to each other like words in the lines of a gigantic book, the bible of my last decade. Some tiles of the roof are covered with green moss, there are wild plants growing from the gutter all along. Some types of weed would grow anywhere just to demonstrate that life finds a way. The weather is making me look at my environment with a new eye, stimulating my curiosity again.

Wally appears from the neighbour's side of the roof, walking comfortably along the gutter as if it was at floor level, he hops onto the terrace, he is tranquilly strolling around, keeping his head up proudly, punctuating his promenade with a stretch, elongating his back legs to make a straight line with his back. A couple of new grown tomatoes are blushing on the side. Wally rubs his side against my leg as he is passing by, i say hi back. I suggest him a chunk of grapefruit and he looks away, aloof, not impressed by the offer. I tell him that grapefruits are full of vitamins that he should try, he is pretending to not even be here. Wally goes and sits close to the edge, wrapping his tail around himself, staring at something i cannot see. "Are you seeing anyone these days?", i ask him. He turns his head to another direction, still ignoring what i am saying, perhaps i am too nosey. The gray, black and white of his tabby coat patterns kind of match with the colours of the bricks that the walls are made of. Maybe that's why he is called Wally. The cat takes advantage of his camouflage and the fact that i'm on the opposite side of the terrace to get inside the door to the warehouse. He goes in slowly until his tail disappears.

A ukulele sound is fleeting in the air, coming from the fire escape outdoor stairs of the six story building on the other side. The quiet breeze carries the melodies, they travel about twenty meters to reach my ears on the red bean bag. I turn and raise my head to see who's playing. It is a guy with long dyed hair, i've seen him before, perhaps on a stage somewhere or at a party but never up on this staircase, he must have moved in recently. You can see all of London from where he is sitting, it makes sense to be looking for ideas there.

The neighbourhood is quite creative, it gathers so many artists and musicians, there would be enough of us in here to complete the line up of a festival stage for a day i reckon. However, the artistic activity has attracted a different type of crowd recently, the type of people that don't seem to understand that everyone is responsible for keeping the vibe alive, that it is not just the matter of putting a few cool posters up. Around the courtyard last night, a party was going, at some point, a bunch of big mouths were getting into a fight, shouting unsophisticated words aggressively, eager to demonstrate their superior levels of testosterone. That brought a change, i usually hear choruses of Fleetwood Mac numbers sung in high pitched drunk voices.

The warehouse at the entrance of the courtyard behind our building has been nicely redone not so long ago, photographers have developed a studio in it. There's another warehouse with photographers around the block, these guys must be more fashion orientated judging by the models who pass by from time to time. There is a small gallery next door that is open weekends only, with a basketball hoop on its wall. The hoop is open every day of the week. This is one side of the road. The other side is mostly council houses, sandwiched by a designer's studio on one end and a music studio on the other. There is a garage and then the back gardens of Haredi Jewish families. One of them has a trampoline, it is Shabbat today and kids are jumping on it with a huge ball. There are new young trees that have been recently planted along the pavement. The road has been revived, some neighbours believe the trees have been mostly put there to please future investors more than locals, nevertheless, they look quite cute. There are lampposts standing along there too, currently sleeping. The back side of the road is made of old cobblestones, they're all polished at the top, perhaps they used to be taller. There is a family of wheelie bins by the entrance of the courtyard and on their side, there is a spot where residents leave pieces of furniture they want to get rid of. I found my desk and a few other discoveries down there before.

There are opinions, like in every neighbourhood, some cohabit, some are borrowed, some are contagious, some provoke others, they influence the life in here even though they're invisible. I'm aware of some of them but not as much now as when i was working at the bakery café. Back then, i used to meet residents from the street at least once a week. There was always food in the café that didn't sell on the day and couldn't be sold the next day so i would fill a bin bag with it, loaves of bread, croissants, pains au chocolat, pains aux raisins, bagels, quiches, sausage rolls and give it away on my way back here. I would give it to beggars, drug addicts or anyone in need that i saw, but most ended up with the people who live on my road. My initial intention was to avoid wastage, i was finding it difficult to trash all that food knowing how some people struggle financially around here. So i would take it as a duty, and with a black bin bag on my back, i would go and meet my neighbours. Interestingly enough, some people from the council houses would find it weird to get something for free without being asked anything in return and would refuse the gift. Apart from them or the ones who are gluten intolerant, my activity was appreciated and thanks to it, i got to know the neighbourhood and, in particular, the starving artists better. They all have opinions about each other, but in my opinion, the neighbourhood would not be the same without such vibrant mixture. It's been a while since i left the bakery. I work in a pub these days but i can't bring booze back, even though i know a few people who would enjoy that.

A bird lands on the side by the plants, another visitor.
It is a magpie.
I'm wondering if magpies eat strawberries, because there are some in the pot nearby that are showing off red colours and i still haven't tried any of these yet this year.
She walks by the berries and continues on her way to the palm tree.
She tries to pull a leaf from the tree with her beak but the tree resists.
She picks up a dried leaf from the floor instead.
She walks back, opens her wings to fly off but drops the leaf as she launches into flight.
She flies to the six story building and lands on the last window sill of the fifth floor empty-clawed.
She jumps onto the pipe just below, takes a few steps and flies back towards me.
She lands near the palm tree and looks for another dead leaf leaning on the pot.
She pulls one, drops it, picks it up again and flies off with

it to the same spot.

She drops the leaf methodically in between the pipe and the wall.

The magpie is building her nest by the black pipe.

Wally has missed this spectacle, i wonder where he is now, perhaps in my room playing with my guitar.

A helicopter crosses the sky, the noise attracts my attention, making me notice the airplanes that are flying even higher. I'm lying on my back, the filling inside the bean bag adapts to the shape of my position, comfitting the lower part of my back that suffers from the many hours standing at the pub. It is hard to stay still, i'm overflowing with energy, i should go for a quick jog at a smooth pace in the sunshine, that'd be delightful, and i'd feel cosy in my skin afterwards with the endorphin high. Running refreshes my mind, oxygenates my blood, increases my endurance, strengthens my heart, builds my muscles, burns my fat, puts me in a good mood and amongst all, it is flying intermittently. I grab the grapefruit peel, head to my bedroom and drop it on my coffee table.

I cover my feet with the type of socks that have a sporty brand logo on each side, the ones i wouldn't wear if i wasn't in a sporty situation. It is probably warm enough to go running topless but i don't like seeing the fat of my tummy bouncing when i run. Running makes me more aware of my growing belly, i totally forget about it when i write or make music. Everything's much simpler in literature, i can just add an 'L' to the fat to get it flat, it is more flattering.

Going down the stairs again, rushed by the eagerness to run, to be active physically, i grab my trainers, they've got a logo on each side too. I am not endorsed by any of the names on my running gear but they want me to inform everyone that i am wearing them.

"Have you seen Wally?" i

"Yeah, i've let him out, i was wondering how he got in actually..." Jude

"He came from the roof, you should have seen him walking on the gutter, fearless" i

"He's cheeky, please let's not let him in anymore, the other night he came to my bedroom and freaked me right out" says Lyla, sliding down the pole from her bedroom to the living room, clenching her legs strongly enough to reduce the speed of her descent, holding her laundry in one hand. I sit on the sofa to lace my running shoes.

"What did the little fucker do?" Jude

"He attacked my feet" Lyla

"Seriously?" Jude

"Remi was there too, i woke up to Wally's claws in my feet, it scared the shit out of me, i made Rémi take him out" Lyla

"Wally must have mistaken your toes for little animals" i

"Why mine and not Rémi's? If mine were as hairy as his, i could understand" Lyla

"Rémi's feet probably look scarier" Jude
"Cats see better at night but can't see things from a close distance, they actually use their whiskers and their smell to interpret what's going on, perhaps your feet reminded him of an edible creature" i
"Oh right, my feet reminded him of cat food" Lyla
"Cat food? Wait, give us a look at your feet Lyla" Jude

Lyla goes towards the table with a funny walk sliding her flip flops on the floor as if they were moving little animals.

"Oh you've got a ring on one of your toes that's why! Cats love fancy feet!" Jude
"Is it a wedding ring? Has Rémi proposed yet?" i
"Yes it is, we got married in a shoe shop, do you mind stopping staring at my feet now?" Lyla

Lacing running shoes is more than knotting pieces of string, lacing running shoes sets my mind to action mode, tying the knot of my tracksuit bottoms never inspires me the same way.

"Alright, in a bit" i
"In a bit" Jude
"In a bit" Lyla

[Vlam!]

The door slams behind me, the noise is reverberating around the walls of the corridor, i add a drumming sound to it with my feet going down the staircase of the building and keep the rhythm going until the front door. Outside, the light makes me squint, accentuating the wrinkles around my eyes. I'm getting into a slow jog, it feels good getting into motion, using up some energy, accelerating my heartbeat slowly. There are asphalt scars on the ground where cobblestones have been removed, looking at them makes me wonder what is happening underground.

This part of the neighbourhood gets completely deserted on Saturdays as it holds one of the biggest Haredi Jewish communities in Europe. The quietness today is overwhelming, the shops are closed, vans and minivans have left the road, buggies have left the pavement along with Yiddish language. Maybe it's the waves of prayer coming from the houses all around but the peacefulness feels spiritual.

There's a busy road to cross before reaching the common, i have to stop and wait for the vehicles to pass when i was just getting into the tempo. Of course i could keep my body moving on the spot like other joggers do but i dislike gesticulating on the pavement without going forward. I am not in a discotheque, i find it stupid, or perhaps i haven't found an angle that allows me to appreciate it intellectually yet. A double decker passes, wearing a number on each of its sides like sportsmen do. As it goes, i pounce on the zebra and keep my flow going to the grass of the common. The road that follows leads to the canal, it is so steep that i usually find impossible to ride it down on a bicycle without using the brakes more than once. I'm trying to maintain a reasonable speed to keep the way down pleasant, if i was built for extreme sports, i would know by now.

There's a guy coming from the opposite side cycling up the hill. He is standing, pushing hard on the pedals, fighting with the slope, he is almost immobile. I am getting faster unintentionally, the more i go down, the more green appears on both sides of the road with Springfield park on the right and a rugby pitch on the left, with an 'H' on each end, like 'hashish', 'high' or 'horseradish'.

Along the canal, there are narrow boats lined up one after another, 'à la queue leu leu' as we say in French. They're all attached to the border with a rope like untrustable dogs, holding plants, bicycles, solar panels, wood and other reserves for the colder times. I take the bridge heading to the wilderness, following the zigs and zags of the path, gravel along the way are bringing noise to my steps, they attract attention to my feet but i want to hear the sound of nature around me.

There's a man, about thirty meters away, who is running in a funny way in my direction. He is dressed like he is training for a marathon or a serious competition but the way he is moving his arms doesn't seem to help his velocity, although if the determination on his face is proportional to his stamina, he might go far. There's a blond girl who follows up, she also has a funny way of running, moving the head as if it was party time, maybe she is exercising her ponytail. These two make me become self conscious about the way i run, my moves could look ridiculous too, hopefully not like these two.

I hear steps coming behind me, someone is going to overtake me, as it often happens with my speed. The steps are getting closer, it is a woman, wearing leggings with a nice derrière, which is my favourite type of person to be overtaken by, a woman with a peachy bum. I guess for some people it must create a satisfying feeling to overtake someone, i'd be glad if it did. I'm not here to compete with anyone nor to get myself overworked. I'm here to enjoy and speed has never been my thing. There is a flock of birds flying above, evolving organically. I am followed by my thoughts, the little derrière is way ahead now.

On the canal, the wildlife is doing its business, swans are walking on water as they are landing. Some other swans are floating upside down with the head in the water and the bottom in the air, i'm wondering if they are fishing or if they are aerating their bum, perhaps it is an excuse to avoid farting in water, the bubbles would clearly look uncool.

Sweat starts emerging, calories are burning. I am taking the next bridge back, it has to be a short run, i don't want to get tired. I've got to go to the pub later to cover a colleague who is working on a film today and i'm also going on a date tonight.
There's a tennis court, a couple is having a ball. I'm running in the park and starting to feel the hill in my legs.

At the top of the slope, the ground is flat like an escalope. My lungs are wide open and i slowed down to a walk. I can see my friend further down in the park, i am going towards it, doing circles with my arms like butterfly swimming in the air. I notice a couple sitting on the grass a little further up and walk more discreetly to my friend to say bonjour.

I have a good friend in Springfield park, a very old one, that has been living there for a long time. I visit it regularly. I come here and share some thoughts with it, it is so calm, it is always of good advice. It usually wears light green foliage with long thin leaves, it has Asian roots, it has quadruple 'U' for initials, it is a Weeping Willow.

This big tree has been there before me and will be there

after me, and because its connections with the sky and the ground are greater than mine, i tend to believe that the tree knows better than i do. It makes sense to me to commune with it because it allows me to be one with nature, to set my mind, my heart and feelings naturally in the purest disposition. Some people have a religion, i have a tree. It is always good to touch wood.

I wish hugging trees was democratised in this part of the world because it really feels good doing it. Usually, when there are people around or passing by, i connect with it more discreetly just by laying my back on it to avoid attracting attention. It is all clear on one side. I walk closer to the tree, step by its roots and open my arms. I can only reach half of its circumference, i stick my chest against its trunk and that is enough to be one with it. I'm disappearing into nature.

Music and showers refresh like no other.

The steam has almost covered the whole mirror, i can only see my legs in it. I've wet the floor whilst stepping out of the shower to grab my shampoo from the shelf. I tried to be quick, walking on the tips of my toes but it is hard to win against water. I shut the turquoise curtain with its pineapple motifs and get back under the stream.

[*On my way to see my friends who lived a couple of blocks away from me ha...*]

Craig David has brightened a good amount of people's summer with this number. I don't know where the inspiration to play it came from earlier, the '7 days' melody popped in my head and was sticking, i had to play it. It is such a fruity track, it goes well with the shower curtain. Like with most songs, i only know a limited amount of the lyrics, the flow here is too fast for me to understand them all anyway but i gather he's having much more sex than me in this one.

My blood cells are partying, the shot of oxygen and endor-phins from the jog makes me feel amazing. The water is running on my chest, i'm pouring shampoo on my left palm, perhaps more than the sufficient amount. Quan-tities in the Western world are approximately excessive, it is the stupid joy of the culture, to imitate adverts. I'm kneading an unnecessary volume of unctuous lather on the top of my head, i must look like a giant q-tip.

[*...and on Thursday & Friday & Saturday we chilled on Sunday...*]

Somehow i have the impression that i have lost some weight but that's probably the empty stomach morning illusion.
Someone must have turned on the tap on the other end of the plumbery. The water is getting colder, i can't com-plain, it is so warm outside.
Looking down to my pelvis area, the pubes zone could do with a summer trim, there's a forest down there. I can't even remember the last time i did it. The cup near the soaps area gathers pink and blue ladies razors but no scissors. There are probably some on the shelf. I'm going out of the shower, wetting the floor again, this time only my feet are visible in the mirror. As i'm near the music player, i take the chance to put on another track as Craig's David's week is nearly over. I want to play 'Ms Fat Booty' by Mos Def but my fingers are dripping.

[*Monday, took her for a drink on Tuesday, we were making*

love by Wednesday...]

Now the floor is all wet, i can take the time to dry my hand on a towel and set up the next track. Euphoric waves are conquering my mood, i am singing, that's also what showers are made for, "I know i can't afford to stop, for one moment, that is too soon to forget".

[*In she came with the same type game, the type of girl giving out the fake cell phone and name, big fame, she likes cats with big things...*]

I'm moving my head to the beat as the song unrolls which doesn't help me to be precise in my frizz chopping process. It is actually risky handling scissors that close to my family jewels, a bit of Hip hop and i'm living dangerously.

[*...ass so fat that you could see it from the front...*]

There is black frizzy hair around my feet, i direct the stream strategically to guide it towards the shower hole. A last splash on my face and i put the shower spout back on the hook, i turn the water off. I wipe dripping drops off my hair, chest and legs like i am dusting off my human outfit and pull the pineapples to the wall. I grab my bathrobe and cover myself with it. The mirror is covered with steam, mist is everywhere. My bathrobe feels almost too warm to wear it. It sponges the shower drops along with the new drops of sweat appearing on my body without minding which one is which. I throw the shower rug on the puddle so nobody slips on it.

Out of the steam, the fresher air of the main room caresses my face so nicely that i could almost imagine a good intention behind it. My stomach is trying to get my attention with gurgling noises as i get back up to my cat nest. My stomach is hungry and it is threatening to send me to a grumpy mood if i don't feed it promptly.

A pair of light blue underwear will do, with a pair of summer trousers. I don't need to think about fashion too much, i'm just going to the shop to buy some food, the first T-shirt of the pile will do, no socks needed, the holes of these slippers will ventilate my feet nicely.

Back down to the cupboard, i grab a banana, i'm opening it from where the stalk is, my African friends proceed from the other end, perhaps the style is down to the side of the equator one comes from.

"Does anybody want anything from the shop?" i
"Oh could you get some garlic please?" Lyla
"I'm sorry but asking a French person to pick garlic is a bit discriminatory" i
"Actually, i wouldn't mind some good cheese too" Lyla
"Could you get me a baguette please?" Jude
"I'm just going to the corner shop, i'm not going to France" i
"Oh come on mate, you could get some camembert huh?" Jude

"Seriously, what do you need?" i

"Just garlic thanks" Lyla

Lyla is Australian, Jude is English, somehow some types of jokes are international, i leave the house in my talking moccasins.

[Vlam!]

Down the spiral of stairs, past the front door, my next door and ground floor neighbour Zelda is setting up a camping chair on the road along the axis of the sun by her front door. She is wearing a summer outfit, not a bikini but a short light dress, her legs are thin and long and very pale.

"Hello mister" Zelda

"Hey how are you? Taking advantage of the weather?" i

"Absolutely, look at the sky, wouldn't you?" Zelda

"It is so nice, i've been for a jog already, it was wonderful" i

"Good on you, i wish i had woken up earlier, i feel like i've missed out already, i was glued to my pillow, i couldn't move this morning" Zelda

"Well, have you had a nice dream at least?" i

"I don't think so, not that i remember, i was so tired, today is my first day off in sixteen days, working ten hours a day, so my plan is to do nothing at all, all day, to recover, but also for the sake of doing nothing" Zelda

"That's a lot of hours" i

"It is a stupid amount of hours, that's the thing with working freelance, you're always tempted to take jobs when they come but tend to forget about the fun times" Zelda

"How long are you off for?" i

"Four days, maybe five actually, that's amazing, oh! And the sun! Look at the sun! I was looking at the sky yesterday and the day before from the office hoping that it would stay like that during my days off but it seems even warmer today, this is just great! It makes me so happy" Zelda

"Yep, it's wonderful, i'm going to the shop, do you need anything?" i

"No thank you, i did my shopping yesterday, see! I planned it all so i don't have to do anything today" Zelda

"Well done, what about sun lotion, did you think of sun lotion?" i

"Are you trying to say that my legs are white Monsieur with Mediterranean skin? No i'm fine thank you, i've got some left over from last summer" Zelda

"Otherwise just put olive oil and let them roast" i

"Roasts are for Sundays so maybe tomorrow!" Zelda

"Bon, let's stop talking about legs, i'm starving, i need to get some food, i see you later" i

"See ya" Zelda

Zelda joined the neighbourhood a few months ago, she is into psychology. I'm not entirely sure what her work is exactly about, i know that she goes to different companies to listen to their employees like councillors do, i guess she is a guide of some sort. Zelda says she is a feminist, she could be a postfeminist too perhaps, she may have a problem with men in general but maybe that's just how i feel when she disses the gender that i am. Zelda has a strong character, i've seen her involved in some heated arguments in the past, for a sexist joke or for a macho move. She wouldn't hesitate to give someone a lecture if this person crossed the borders of her principles. Sometimes, the way she talks about men makes me wonder if she actually could date any, but as this is a personal question and as she can be pretty tough, i never dared asking.

Walking by the houses towards the main road, the ginger tomcat is laying on his ledge as usual. His name is Spartacus. Spartacus is probably older than Wally and he is rarely seen on the other part of the road. Me and him never really connect much but still, i always say hello.

There is a wall at the entrance of the street that is always covered with graffiti, two street artists from the neighbourhood usually take care of it. Somehow, it is allowed to paint on that wall and not the others. The orange cat Garfield is a character that appears often on this wall, drawn in different situations, he is there at the entry of the road with his paws opened, inviting anyone to give him a high five. Today, they are painting something in black and white on the other end of the wall. They are currently designing the letters of a French word which makes me want to go talk to them. The drawing is pretty minimal, it pictures a dog in a room, an opened door, an unattached leash left on the floor near an empty dog bowl. The French phrase in big letters says: 'OH LA VIE' which means:'OH LIFE' and the other part in smaller characters says: 'Qu'est ce que je ferais sans toi' which means: 'What would i do without you', so i go ask the guys what's up.

"Hey, sorry to interrupt, i always appreciate your work on that wall but it is the first time i see you guys writing something in French on it, so it pushes me to ask you what is the reason behind it? Any special occasion?" i

"Nice one man, sure yeah, well basically, we both have a French girlfriend, and so we wanted to make a little homage" street artist 1

"Oh that's nice, brave men, i always respect guys who venture with a French woman, i've been there before, i know how challenging it can be" i

"Ha true! But doesn't it make things more interesting?" street artist 1

"Hang on" i

"What?" street artist 1

"I think there is a grammatical issue" i

"Where?" street artist 1

"I think the 's' at the end of 'ferais' shouldn't be there..." i

"Really? Are you sure?" street artist 2

"Well, i believe so but wait, i can be a bit dyslexic sometimes so let me see what the internet says" i

"Yes please" they say, adding little touches of paint to the wall.

"That's it look, 'Je ferai', see?" i say, showing the screen of my phone.

"That's right, oh nice one man, that's a good thing, i didn't like the look of that 's' anyway" street artist 2

"Thanks for telling us man, appreciate it" street artist 1

"Yeah thank you man" street artist 2

"No worries" i reply and leave happily, appreciating the satisfaction i get from my cultural contribution to my road.

The traffic on the main road is quite hectic, the noise of London's hustle and bustle reappears here and reminding me that i live in a big city. The pavement is quite large, i guide my steps towards the corner shop where i'll get eggs and garlic. A youngster is riding his bike super fast on the footway, i feel the rush of air as he passes so close to me, his lack of concern makes me moan. Inside the barbershop, two men are sitting on a chair with white foam on their face. There's a woman in a short red dress just outside the kebab shop, she is smoking a cigarette elegantly, probably waiting for a shish to cook, she's looking at her phone, moving her thumb actively on it. Two bicycles are left on the floor just by the entrance of the shop, i enter, two youngsters are at the counter talking in their street slang to Hassan the manager of the shop. There is a buzzing noise coming from the speakers where the radio is played, it has been there for the past weeks. It sounds like it is stuck in between frequencies, in somewhere foggy between two radio stations. I reach the egg section, it looks emptier than usual, there are only boxes of cheap eggs, i look around and get back to the counter. The youngsters leave with their gangster attitudes, Hassan smiles at me, starting to impersonate them, he is pumped up with energy like always.

"Are you a real G?" Hassan

"Not sure actually, are you?" i

"Bruv, i'm not a G, i am a G spot finder, the finest kind of G, you get me?" Hassan

"G-nius" i

"Yeah bruv, gynecolo-G, the pengest G of Hackney, you get me?" Hassan

"Big man ting, what about the E-double G? How come you don't have any eggs today? Where have they all gone?" i

"What are you talking about? There are eggs, look" Hassan

"But these ones come from caged chicken, i want free range ones" i

"It's the same, organic or not, it's eggs, i guarantee you there is yellow in them, try them, if there's no yellow, i pay you back" Hassan

"I can't consciously eat caged eggs, it makes me feel like i am caged myself" i

"But bruv it doesn't matter, everyone is caged, look at me, do you know how many hours i spend in this shop? You get me? Look, it is so sunny today, i'd love to go out but still, i have to stay here you get me?" Hassan

"I get you, bon, i'm gonna have a look at the super-market" i

"You do that, but we should have some soon so come

back, don't give your money to the big corporations,
give it to your local businesses, you know we're good"
Hassan
"I know you are" i
"Good man, au revoir" Hassan
"Güle güle" i

Walking up the street, marking a pause by the pedestrian traffic light, waiting until the traffic stops and the
red walking lad turns green. The tall guy standing on the
other side of the crossing must have pressed the button
already, the 'WAIT' light is on. He is wearing purple hair
with colourful makeup, he is dressed like an old woman, old spinster style, but he probably doesn't appreciate
being called 'he'. I am thankful this person has informed
the lights. More people are gathering and cars are slow-
ing down, the switch is imminent.

The doors of the supermarket open as i walk towards
them, they can detect my presence. It is nice of the
shop to show some sensitivity, it allows me to prolong
my stream of thoughts without having to worry about
anything. It engulfs me like a whale yawning under the
sea. Metallic baskets are piled up, one into another, steel
against steel, spooning each other, building mini towers
by the entrance. Cashiers are aligned one behind another playing beep sounds, an unpleasant sensation of cold
is trying to spoil my mood. The temperature difference
from outside and here makes my skin react, goosebumps
appear, poultryesque, i just need to get chicken eggs.

All these sections, filled up with products, all arranged strategically with colourful tags to attract attention. Price ranges and expiry dates, ingredients and carefully designed logos, packagings and offers, positioning and lighting, everything has been thought so carefully to anticipate my human behaviour. Apart from the temperature difference from the weather outside. Air conditioning should be more tolerant, no one should be shocked by a climate change when wanting to buy six eggs. I'm walking faster, luckily i don't need anything refrigerated. I'm passing by the bread section, realising i need bread too and that i should have thought of that when i was at the corner shop as their bread tastes better. If i go through another section, i may find more needs that i didn't think of. It's cold and i'm hungry, let's focus on that, i should never go food shopping on an empty stomach.

Eggs.
Organic eggs.
Opening a box.
Checking the way the eggs look, a small feather is stuck to one of them, reminding me of where they come from.
Closing the box.
Taking the box.
Walking towards the cashiers, the ones with humans, not the self checkout.
Estimating the queues by number of people and amount of products on conveyor belt.
Joining a queue.
Waiting.

Picking up the phone, diving into the internet.

Loading wheel spinning.

Refusing to wait on another platform as the point was to escape from waiting.

Locking up the phone.

My ears get attracted by a familiar sound. There's a music i know on the supermarket radio. It is by the band of my friend Bart. I discovered that song during the time when it was being written. It is interesting to notice how it has traveled from a bedroom guitar to a supermarket. It sounds a bit cheesy, it should only be played in the dairy section. It makes me smile to hear it in here. Last time i listened to that song, i was wearing muddy wellies and a waterproof poncho. I was floundering in different kinds of high with my friend Leo at Glastonbury festival when Bart played it live with his band. The supermarket DJ interrupts the song, saying that someone is needed on cashier number 12.

There is a packet of crumpets in the pile of items of the customer ahead of me. I'm thinking that if i swap the 'c' of 'crumpets' with a 't' i would get 'trumpets'. It makes me search for other cases such as 'cable' and 'table' or 'coast' and 'toast'. Self-entertainment is quite useful whilst queuing, i'm trying to find more possibilities but here comes my turn.

On the conveyor belt, my eggs are moving to my friend's music. I acknowledge the woman at the till, she replies without much attention as she takes my box of eggs and scans it under x rays. She looks preoccupied but still asks me if i own or wish to acquire the loyalty card of the supermarket and a five pence bag. I decline the offers assuming the egg box will be enough to carry the eggs until home and conclude that i don't need to be loyal to the supermarket. She gives me the total amount and i decide to pay by card. I insert my credit card into the card machine. It is a quick in and out, i am not trying to fuck the system. I wish her a good day, she's already talking to the next customer, it must be the temperature inside the shop that made her behave so coldly.

"Hey the cat!"

Someone is shouting behind me as i pick up my freshly bought item, it is Liam. 'Liam' is not his real name but everyone calls him Liam because he looks and talks like Liam Gallagher. "Liam, please don't make me jump when i'm holding eggs, how are you doing?" i say. He smiles between his sideburns, his girlfriend Siobhan is walking behind him, she is on the phone, i high five him and wave at her.

"Y'alright man? Looking good, what're you up to? Fancy coming to ours for brunch? We've got the lads over from back home, my cousin's here, good times, i'm buzzing man" Liam
"Nice, thanks but i think i'm gonna stick to the plan of making myself an omelette, probably stick to the pan too, i'm starving, need to get that out of the way as quick as possible, are you going to cook?" i

"That's it, a bit of brunch for the missus and the lads d'you know i mean? Check out this weather man, it looks like Miami or some sunny arse town, good job i'm not wearing fucking long johns d'you know i mean? Gagging!" Liam

I laugh, Liam sounds like he hasn't slept yet, i can't really tell by his eyes as he is wearing sunglasses but the smell of alcohol coming from his breath and clothes tell me that he must have had a big one. The traffic lights turn green as we're walking towards them, making us feel special somehow.

"That's what i call timing! Oh man, i'm roasting, i tell you one thing, if London was sunny like this all the time, i'd have to live elsewhere d'you know i mean? I couldn't handle it, i'd have to build a focking fan to blow on me face constantly, i'd look like a focking science fiction idiot, blimey, i'm sweating like planet Mars man" Liam

"Like planet Mars?" i

"Yeah man, have you not heard? They've found water on it, the thing is alive" Liam

"Sweaty ball" i

"Yeah that's it, a big focking sweaty ball, like the pair i've got between me legs, the ones she busts, drop the phone love, it's the weekend! She is not listening, addicted to that focking phone like focking junkie, oh man, i'm gonna cook brunch, i'm telling you it's going to be more special than The Specials, my cousin is here, what a legend this one is, have you met my cousin Ray?" Liam

"Is he the one with the lion tattoo?" i

"Lion tattoo?" Liam

"The one who plays Reggae" i

"Ah no, that's Rob, Rob's not family, if he was, i'd have to sue my parents, the boy is a nutta" Liam says as he throws a plastic packaging of a Mars barre on the floor, not so far away from a litter bin.

"Were you aiming at that bin?" i

"Haha no i wasn't" Liam

"Why not?" i

"Mate, it creates jobs d'you know i mean? If i put it in the bin, someone is going to lose a job, you have to think for everyone d'you know i mean?" Liam

"That's generous of you" i

"Fact" Liam

"Merde! I was going to forget the bread, sorry i gotta go to that shop" i

"A baguette? Of course, well i'll see you later, come over for a brew, give us a shout if you're about" Liam

"Ok, another time" i

"So long the cat!" Liam

I pace it back to the shop, i wish i could walk as slowly as Liam but my stomach is pushing me. Hassan looks surprised to see me entering his shop again, i go straight to the bread section, grab an already sliced loaf with seeds, get back to him and lay a two pounds coin on the counter.

"You again? You came back quicker than i expected"
Hassan

"Is it not annoying hearing that noise all day?" i

"What noise?" Hassan

"From the radio, the buzzing sound" i

"Oh the radio! I think there's a problem with the anten-
na, we can't fix it" Hassan

"Are you sure?" i

"I'm not sure but i don't listen to it anyway" Hassan

"Ok, see you later, please give the change to the kids" i
say, pointing to the charity box for the children in need.

Back outside, the barbers still look busy and so are the
graffiti artists drawing their dog. The sun is leading the
way, the rarity of the weather conditions should be appreciated more, i must try to control my hunger instead of
walking hurriedly. I slow down and take a deep breath. I
exhale slowly and repeat the action two more times until
my mind understands that i can deal with the situation
without involving stress. Naturally, the hunger retreats.
The result makes me content, i keep on walking more
relaxed down the road, appreciating the benefits of my
physical intervention. Closer to my door, Zelda is fully set
up in her camping chair with a beer in one hand and a
doobie in the other, she is blazing on it. The smoke comes
out of her mouth making the air opaque around her head.
Her housemate Renee has joined her, she is laying on a
big cushion horizontally so she can capture more of what
the sky is offering. The two neighbours have their legs
out, they're wearing sunglasses, i can hardly tell what

they are looking at or if even their eyes are opened.

Renee is from Birmingham, i've been told once that her first name is Priscilla but as she doesn't like it, she usually introduces herself by her second name Renee. Renee has a deep voice, she can get really rude when she is drunk and when she does, her timbre and choice of words work well together. The first time i met Renee, she was smashed and was insulting me for being French. She just moved into the neighbourhood a couple of months ago, she's been ok with me coming from France since we talked about it, i think.

"It smells nice out here, i see you're quite productive for someone who didn't want to do anything all day" i
"I'm allowing myself to roll and open cans, it's the minimum i can do, maybe i'll cook later but no guarantees" Zelda
"Hi Renée" i
"Hello" Renee
"Would you like a puff?" Zelda asks me handing the spliff in my direction.
"Oh no, thank you, i'd rather go for calories, otherwise i'm going to faint" i
"Say hello to mister Frenchman" Renee says pulling a green animal out of her cleavage.
"What!? What the f is this?!" i ask as i pounce back.
"It's mister Zigg, oh yes, mister Zigg is happy today isn't he?" Renee says, petting her animal between her breasts, talking to it as if it was a baby, kissing its

mouth as it is pointing its head out of her boobs.

"What is it?" i

"Mister Zigg is a lizard" Zelda

"Do you have a lizard as a pet?" i

"Yeah, it's like a baby chameleon but it doesn't change colour, he's always green" Renee says, somehow managing to turn her deep voice into a cute sound, she adds, "Mister Zigg has his space in my room, we live together, like a happy couple".

"I didn't know lizards were pettable, i mean, don't they like climbing walls and stuff? Does he not wander off? How do you keep him? He's not on a leash is he?" i

"No, no leash needed, he stays with me, he's got his beautiful cage in my bedroom, he loves it, look at him, isn't he well here? Who wouldn't like staying between a pair of tits, look he's all cosy... Oh! Baby stay here! don't go down on me, not in front of everybody..." Renee shouts as Mister Zigg is crawling down her tank top, going towards her shorts.

"Mister Zigg is pretty naughty" i

"He's scared of you" Zelda

"No he's not, he's just feeling horny that's all" i

"Darling, it's not only about sex, you Frenchmen see lust everywhere" Zelda

"Look at him, he's going for it" i

"He's hiding from your dirty French mind" Renee

"My mind is not dirty, i've actually cleaned it this morning" i

"Really? And how did you clean it? With detergent, what type? I'm curious" Zelda

"With savon de Marseille, no, i've done a bit of medi-tation" i

"Mindfulness! Good on you, how long did you meditate for?" Zelda

"I don't know, ten minutes? Maybe five, i'm not sure" i

"You should aim for twenty, twenty minutes is a good amount. If everyone meditated for twenty minutes everyday, there would be peace on earth" Zelda

"It's hard though, not to think, i find it quite difficult to focus on the breathing, calming down the thinking process" i

"It's good to practice, you should keep on doing it, it'll get easier, although even five minutes is a good start" Zelda

"Not enough for a Frenchman" Renee

"Thanks, but hey, it'd make sense to me if Mister Zigg would get horny by this type of weather, it's not being sleazy saying this, it is quite a natural thing" i

"It's because you're French, did you hear that Mister Zigg? Mmh don't listen to mister Frenchman, you're my baby, oh you're so cute" Renee

"Cute? Really? I've never heard anyone using the word 'cute' with a lizard before" i

"Maybe not all lizards but Mister Zigg is so cute, look at him!" Zelda

"Don't listen to him Mister Zigg, the Frenchman is so rude, of course you're cute" Renee says as she kisses Mister Zigg on the mouth again.

"You look disgusted, what's the trouble?" Zelda

"But does he not...? i

"Does he not what?" Renee

"Forget about it, i'm just hungry, it must affect my perception, i need to eat something, i see things differently after an omelette, it is the first time i see someone kissing a lizard you know, it is surprising to me" i

"It is quite a natural thing!" Renee says, doing an impression of me, like the way i said it earlier.

"Well, i better go on with my omelette, i've got a few eggs waiting to be beaten" i say and walk towards the entrance of the building.

"You do that, see you later" Zelda

"Enjoy the sunshine! Bye Mister Ziggy!" i

"Bye Mister Frenchman" says Renee holding and waving the tiny arm of her lizard.

Up the stairs, i open the door, a smell of food tickles my nose, i can't tell what's cooking but it smells appetising. Gingembre has come back from wherever she was earlier, she could have been to a hundred different places already this morning, her energy is just incomparable. Gingembre has red hair, hence the nickname i gave her. 'Gingembre' is French for 'Ginger', i haven't been able to call her by her real name since this association clicked in my mind, and as she likes it and speaks a bit of French, i keep on using it. It also suits her passion for cooking, it adds some spice at least.

Amongst the seven of us, Gingembre is the one who has lived in the warehouse the longest. I moved in a few years ago, the five others joined after. There was a big turnover two years ago and since then, it is the same bunch of people living here. Gingembre kind of represents the authority, she is the one in charge of keeping a good standard in the place. Gingembre is a food critic, she is often creating around the stove and everyone gets to try her experiments. She has blue eyes that are shaped like cat's eyes and when she adds mascara to them i would almost expect her to talk in meows. I don't think she is aware of the power her charm has on me, especially when she speaks in French with her British accent. If we didn't live together, i would have probably let myself succumb. I am glad we reached the friend zone without complications, dating a housemate would be too problematic, i am too attached to my freedom. I'd rather look at her as if she was a sister so the attraction disappears, like i always do with women i shouldn't project myself with. It is the best way i found to trick magnetism, to stop sexual intentions without taking away the enjoyment of being in woman's company. It works for me wonders and thanks to this, i've always been comfortable with her presence despite the influence of her obvious charm. It feels great living with her, seeing her almost everyday, her spontaneity always takes me off guard and i couldn't find a big enough scale to measure her generosity. Her energy is just incomparable.

"Bonjour Gingembre" i

"Bonjour petit choux fleur" Gingembre

"What are you making?" i

"I'm baking a courgette cake" Gingembre

"A cake with courgettes? Seriously?" i

"Yep, comment tu dis en français, 'la courgette'? Ou 'la zucchini'?" Gingembre

"We say 'courgette', 'un gâteau à la courgette', what inspired you to make a gâteau à la courgette?" i

"I have never done a gâteau à la courgette before and

as courgettes are in season, i thought i should give it a go" Gingembre

"What other vegetables are you putting in it?" i ask whilst washing my hands in the sink in between her cooking tools.

"Just courgettes, it is not a ratatouille" Gingembre

"Oh garlic!" i

"I am not putting garlic in it" Gingembre

"No, i was meant to get garlic but i completely forgot, it just comes back to me" i

"Oh don't worry i bought some earlier" She grabs a garlic bulb, takes a clove off and hands it to me.

"Brilliant, thanks, what would i do without you Gingembre?" i

"What would you do without garlic?" Gingembre

"Actually the garlic was for Lyla but i am going to use some in my omelette" i

"Of course" Gingembre

Visitors often ask how it is to live with so many people at the warehouse. There are only four rings of stove for seven adults, only one shower and two toilets, one oven and only one washing machine. For people who are used to living on their own or as a couple, it can be hard to perceive the comforts and the lifestyle that a place like that can provide. How to have intimacy? How to deal with everyone's moods and differences? What if someone is dirty? Or noisy? Or sad? Or drunk? How do you share the tasks? Who cleans? Can you invite people over? Who chooses the music? What if someone else wants to listen to something different or doesn't like what is played? What if you want to be on your own or walk naked in the living room? What if you're feeling bad and you don't feel like talking to anyone? What if you come back from work tired and someone is having a party? Do you hear your housemates having sex? Do you hang out together all the time? Do you all eat together and cook for each other? What if someone is vegan or vegetarian and someone is cooking meat? How do you decide what TV program to watch?

The short answer to these is, beyond having only one shower, four stoves or one washing machine, there is one love, and one love can gather a lot of people.

Of course, to live this lifestyle, one has to learn how to live with others. One has to know how to wait if the cooker or the shower are busy. Sometimes the washing machine can provoke a little queue, sometimes the fridges get crammed and everyone's energy doesn't always match but more or less, it all works out organically. Everyone has different schedules, everyone eats and showers at different times, it just works out naturally. Sometimes we make a big dinner together and everyone contributes with a side dish or wine but it is actually difficult to gather all the housemates at the same time, such an operation would have to be planned in advance or to happen by some spontaneous miracle. Obviously, intimacy is reduced and if walking naked is someone's thing, they can always do it in their bedroom. The general atmosphere of the place depends on everyone's mood so it is everyone's responsibility to keep it vibrant and inspiring. Usually, if someone is a bit down, or if a problem of some sort occurs, Gingembre would know how to revive the vibe or to dig into the problem to help resolve it. She has set a standard, she raises the barre and makes sure nobody stays too far away from it. The standard leads and encourages everyone to live in harmony with it. Sometimes Gingembre does what she calls a 'fridge patrol', inspecting the products in the fridges that are expired and throwing them away. Once, she binned one of my cheeses, thinking it was off. It was obviously a different assessment than mine and i had to explain the cultural difference to her. Dialogue is always a helper, it is more than that actually, dialogue is a blessing in such space living with so many people. It is enriching, there's so much to learn from each other's culture.

We have a cleaner who comes every other week and who cleans the common areas, he makes more money per hour than i do at the pub when he is cleaning our space. I never wanted his job though.

It is fair to say that toilets and anything that requires a certain amount of hygiene can bring issues when people are not trained to be clean. It is quite difficult to explain the basics of hygiene to anyone, no one likes to be taught about these things at an adult age. Regardless of the social background, hygiene seems to only be learned at a young age, people who grew up one way don't appear to be motivated to change. Hygiene is a form of respect, but some people don't see it that way. Educating to a standard can be a tough job as it is not easy to say these things. Fortunately Gingembre has enough character to express herself on any matter.

Regarding the choice of music, it is never a worry when you have a housemate who has a great record collection and who likes to buy vinyls regularly. It is a bit more difficult with radio, because of the adverts and the news, fortunately headphones can sort this problem out. But there can also be the usual situation with music, when the evening is spontaneously turning into a party and someone who has had too many drinks wants to play a song several times in a row, not realising it was already embarrassing the first time. Too much alcohol is enemy to most systems anyway, i learnt how to deal with it, and with my new bar experience, i'm getting much better at it every day.

Regarding sex, it can be a bit tricky because of the thinness of the walls. When someone brings a partner home, it can happen that, in the fever of the action, some erotic noises come out of the bedroom. Personally, i don't mind them and as i am the one who stays up the latest, i'm the most inclined to hear these noises, but once again, headphones sort this situation quite easily and it is always nice knowing someone is having sex at home. Sex makes people happy and happiness is beneficial to everyone.

There are no arguments over TV channels selection or remote control as we don't own a TV. I actually wonder who owns a TV in any of the warehouses around. I don't know any artist who does. Also, considering the size of Haredi Jewish community living in the neighbourhood who don't own a television, this problem is just not a problem in our area.

For food, some people hate the smell of fish, some others are disgusted to see meat in a pan but everyone gets over it quickly as it is a primary need.

Olive oil in pan, tanning crushed garlic clove
Adjusting volume of the fire knob with love
Breaking and beating eggs in a glass bowl
With a fork and grease from the elbow
Chopping black olives into bits
Adding them to the beats
They'll act like salt, i act like a rapper
Like a default i grind pepper
Slide two bread slices in the toaster
Whilst the garlic's on the roaster
I come back to the pan attracted by the scent
Grab the bowl and empty the whole content
On the hot flat surface
Mixture's in da place
Cooking, i boost up the flames
Now my finger aims
To the spatula in the cutlery drainer
So many holes in that container
I hear the bread popping
Begging for a topping
I lift the edges so they don't stick
Slide under like Mister Boombastic
I flip the half over, it wasn't that hard
Let's have the omelette with a bit of mustard

In a continuous motion, i take a plate, grab the toasts, lay them on it and lay the omelette on them. I get some cutlery, fill up a pint glass of water and walk up the stairs to the roof leaving Gingembre to her cake activities. Lyla is lying on the red bean bag in the sun, reading a book behind sunglasses. I grab a chair and sit at the table, she wishes me a 'bon appétit'. I realise, as i thank her that i have forgotten to take the mustard. It is too late, the omelette's attraction is too strong, i can't leave the plate.

A garlic olive omelette is possibly the easiest thing to cut, it is even softer than butter. However, the difficulty remains in the regulation of the speed of eating when hunger is calling for food. I try to slow down and appreciate more what i am doing. The crunch of the toasted bread and the softness of the omelette make a combination that easily pleases my very basic expectations. When really hungry, even a garlic olive omelette can taste amazing.

The water acts like a divine intervention, every gulp becomes a blessing. I tilt my head to the sun again, closing my eyes so i don't sneeze. I take a moment to appreciate the feeling of the omnipotent warmth. It is inside, like a prayer, it soothes my inner cosmos. I stay there for a few sighs. I reopen and the colours are a bright mess until my pupils adapt to the intensity of the light. I'm scanning the horizon, looking at the sea of roofs, the noise of Lyla's page turning is stroking my hearing. A couple of birds land on the rooftop, they are hitting the tiles frantically with their beak as if it was a typewriter. They're flying off, i'm zooming back to the palm tree, contemplating its cool silhouette. Lyla grabs her glass of water and downs it sip by sip, breathing in between, the sun has slowed everything down.

"Do you think the palm tree will survive?" i

"Mmh, it's hard to tell, it looks like it's got less leaves than when you brought it up doesn't it?" Lyla

"It does yeah, i suppose the ones that were nearly dead fell off quicker, and actually some must have gone with the help of feathered creatures i've noticed earlier" i

"What do you mean?" Lyla

"I've seen a magpie trying to pull one leaf off the tree to build her nest over there" i

"Really? At least, they're being used for a good cause, for baby birds" Lyla

"Yeah, it actually gives more sense now to why i brought it up here" i

"Maybe it needs a bigger pot" Lyla

"Do you reckon?" i

"This one looks cool but i don't know if the size is right, so maybe yeah" Lyla

"Mmh yeah probably" i

"And some water if the weather stays like this for a few more days" Lyla

"That'd be great, i've almost forgot what is a real sunny summer, somehow it is only when it's back that i remember how much i have been missing it" i

"What a day, i can't remember it being this tropical in

74

London" Lyla
"Some would say it is because of global warming" i
"They would indeed" Lyla
"Does it make you feel nostalgic about Australia?" i
"Funny you should say that, it was snowing at my par-
ents when i called them earlier" Lyla
"Really?" i
"Quite a lot actually, they're loving it" Lyla
"Some would say it is because of global warming" i
"They would indeed" Lyla

I grab my plate and cutlery from the table to go back in, a
noise from a big car accelerating in the street resonates
then slows down abruptly. We can hear Zelda shouting at
the driver, "Where the fuck do you think you are?! This is
a quiet street! You're driving like a fucking moron! There
are kids walking around you idiot! Get out of here with
your stupid car! I just can't believe that! Fuck off!".

"She is a psychologist, she knows how to talk to people" i
say to Lyla as i get back in. Lyla stands up, her curiosity
is stronger than her will to chill. I walk down the stairs
with my plate in hand and get to the sink. Gingembre
is whisking dough with a food mixer, the noise of the
machine is bouncing on the walls, she is looking at me
with her hands on the machine, miming 'sorry about the
noise' with her mouth. I reply with a 'no worries' mime
and wash the fat off the dishes.

I'm having a handful of nuts and the last piece of cake

that remains on the table that Gingembre had made a couple of days ago. Since she is making a new one, there is no guilt in taking it. I down a large glass of filtered tap water, clean and dry the cake plate and put it back on the table smiling at Gingembre, meaning that the courgette one will be welcome there too.

It is quite early, it'd be good to do some music work before going to work. There is this spoken word piece that i started developing the other night, about things i've seen on dating apps. There is so much content on there, like descriptions, choices of pictures or ways of posing that got me inspired, although it is quite hard to write lyrics without sounding horrible towards the other gender and humans in general. Still, i like the idea, i'm playing JAY-Z's instrumental of his 'Girls, Girls, Girls' song and i'm rapping over it. So far i only practiced it quietly, whispering in my room to not wake up my housemates as i've only been working on it at night. Let's try out the lines at a normal volume. I've got my notes ready on the side, i press play and the instrumental goes.

[*woo baby*]
"Swiping like a bartender, love me tender, left, right sliding my finger, surprise like Kinder
Caroline's pouting on her pics, squeezing in her cheeks, promoting lipsticks and behind sunglasses, watches flashes shining on her lips

Like hieroglyphs, Anna says it all with only emojis, jeez,
Louise likes her dungarees,
Ice cream, pizza and cuddle expert, she also says she never
wears skirts,
Looking for the true gentleman, for a non smoker in the
big smoke
Pam's into hula hoop, Tam's into food, books, gym and gin
and tonic, dancing, listening to music
Liz mostly shows selfies, she works at Selfridges but doesn't
sell fridges, she loves spending evenings watching series
Ella loves yoga and travelling, Gaga and modelling, she
does headstands and extends her legs to mime letters
with her friends, i think they're trying to make LOVE with
L.O.V.E., "Hello, it's me, petite brunette who's new in the
city, looking for friendship plus more, wherever mi amor"
Lucy is holding the tower of Pisa with one hand, she only
dates tall men, no time wasters, no one night stand
Scarlet's into literature, she is a teacher, not a cheater
and you have to guess who she is amongst the ones on the
pictures
Sophie seems sophisticated, Katie provocative, Eve is by a
nice car, Carla is a DJ, Jenny comes from Lester, Ester from
America, Erica seems funny, Nicky, Vicky, Becky are really
not keen on hookups, no hookups nor hiccups
Emma talks about her boobs, she says they are real and so
you should be too, she doesn't like tattoos, no champagne
no gain, not impressed like Shania Twain, she moved to
London but doesn't like the rain, it would be a plus if you
come from Spain
Lily's face's hidden, just her phone features, because she

chooses to show pictures of her taking pictures..."

Mmmh, i'm not feeling it.

It sounds pretty bad out loud.

Last night it seemed cool but today it really sounds wack.

I guess my imagination was filling the gaps when i was whispering the text.

I don't think it is for me after all, i can be quite jazzy but i am defo not JAY-Z.

I don't feel the vibe when i express it at normal volume.

It is a bit of a disappointment.

I thought the idea was good though.

Maybe it is for someone else.

Or perhaps it would be funnier if a woman would do a version about men's profiles. I'm sure some guys must come up with some crazy pictures and definitions of themselves too.

Oh well, let's forget about it.

It's ok, it was just an idea.

Or maybe it is just not working today.

Probably not, it was really not working. I can tell it is not for me.

It doesn't matter, it was fun writing it.

My laptop is asking me to download the newest software version. It's been a couple of weeks that it's been asking, i don't know how to tell it that i'm fine with this version, it is becoming embarrassing. It is a bit like when my email service is insisting on asking for my mobile number, for safety reasons apparently, embarrassing. I'm wondering if it inquires for women's number the same way. I can't imagine myself or any guy on the street asking a woman for her number for safety reasons. I am pretty sure that, for safety reasons, the woman wouldn't give her number away. It is interesting how the web is assuming that it can be trusted more than a human being. It makes sense though, i share so much of my intimacy with it already that it must assume i consider it as a close member of my entourage.

'Gone surfing, will be back in half an hour or more.'

Some websites want me to prove that i'm not a robot, now i need to prove to a robot that i am not a robot.

Opening windows, trying to get some fresh air, clicking on one social networking site. This one gathers the profile of some of my friends, people i met once, ex-work colleagues, musicians i played with, women i used to fancy, people i met at school, people i only met once long time ago or even some family members. Scrolling down the feeds amongst posts and comments like it was a newspaper.

Someone is saying that she won't go to a famous store anymore but doesn't say why. I'm guessing she is expecting someone to ask what happened.

Someone has lost his phone, he is suggesting to be

contacted there.

Someone is planning a road trip in Europe and is asking for recommendations.

Someone is inviting people to join her Yoga class today.

Three people have posted the same political video.

Someone is suggesting to go to the concert of his band tonight.

Someone is showing what he is having for lunch.

Someone is on holiday, lying on a beach, showing a blue sea in the background behind her feet, saying that it is a hard day at the office today.

Someone is complaining about the train.

Someone has posted something very personal, perhaps a bit too personal.

Someone is commenting about a TV program he is currently watching, a few people are reacting, they all seem very moved by it.

Someone is showing pictures of her baby again.

Someone has changed his profile picture and looks

almost self-confident on it.

It is the fifth post i see about the weather today in London, i click 'like' on almost all of them.

There are no posts about football, the season must be over.

Out of that platform, clicking onto a different one, i go surfing from one video to another, the wave is endless.

My laptop is breathing out loud, getting so warm on my lap, i'm buffering. The wave has lead me to a point where i am watching bad videos. Bad videos are a signal to inform me i should stop being in front of my computer. I shut it down and place it onto my coffee table near the grapefruit peel from earlier. I've got plenty of time before my shift at the pub. I could walk to work, feel the ground under my feet, feel the sun and air on my face. I could do a detour by Gillett Square, perhaps a couple of friends could be skateboarding there at this hour. I could capture something of this sunny day. I could jot a few notes down about London in the summer. I could just be outside.

Standing up, tilting my head down under the slanted ceiling, i swap my T-shirt for a shirt, taking the 'T' off. I button the shirt up, roll the sleeves up my arms and walk down to my studio space. I grab the cardigan that is near my oldest keyboard and hesitate for a moment. It seems quite pointless to take an extra layer but i don't know where life could take me tonight after the date. I'm not working tomorrow, i am single, i am free, anything is possible. I lay the cardigan on my forearm and notice dust on the keys of my keyboard so i blow on them and cover them with the towel that was meant to cover them. I slip into a pair of moccasins, a fresher pair than my slippers even though i bought these second hand. I grab the door keys, wallet, tobacco, lighter, phone and cram my pockets with it all. I salute everyone in the communal space and follow my ambition.

The door, the staircase, the front door, the neighbours lying under their sunglasses, the smoke, the road, the ginger cat, the freshly finished graffiti, the main road, the red double deckers queuing up at the bus stop, the closed Jewish shops, the Muslim shops, the traffic lights, the cyclists, the Turkish restaurants, the Carribean restaurants, the multitude of cars, the free cash points, the stinky fishmonger, the post office, i walk this way almost every day, but today it looks completely different. Locals have changed, the décor is brighter, the colours are revived, it is all transformed by the weather. There are skirts and dresses floating above the pavement, it is quite beautiful to see. I am quietly humming improvised summer ballades, interpreting the bright metamorphosis of my environment.

Suddenly, my left foot catches against a bump in the pavement, making my melody skip. For a second i get the impression the whole street has witnessed this odd move. It takes me a couple of smoother steps to beat paranoia and bring my feelings back to equilibrium.

The harmony between temperature and fresh breeze is just delightful, it is making my stroll lighter, i'm enjoying the walk until the noise of someone's heels behind me starts to bother my tranquility. The speed of the 'tic tac' sound is out of step with my own, a little more impatient. I slow down to let the person go ahead so i can be at peace with my own tempo, without having to hear a fast metronome pulsing in the background.

I notice, as the metronome proudly overtakes me, that her skirt is caught between her handbag and her hip and a part of her derrière is visible. It is rather humorous seeing her passing by with such attitude and not being aware of the situation. It makes me realise that wearing a short skirt must be quite a job, always having to keep it down, having to be careful when sitting or when standing up, always having to remember not to spread the legs, having the reflex to catch it quickly when the wind blows. The more i think about it, the more i appreciate the effort women do to bring such delight for the eyes. I feel like i should go tell her about her curtain being up but i am hesitating. It is a bit like telling someone they've got something stuck between their teeth, it usually provokes awkwardness despite the good intention. She is also going to think that i've been observing her bottom, my accent is not going to help. I suppose it would be better if it was a woman telling her but i can't see anyone going in her direction apart from me. I will have to face her reaction, that is the price to pay for a good deed sometimes. I need to find the best way to put it and to be quick, i flick through ideas:

"Excuse me, i really don't mean to disturb you but i believe you would appreciate if someone would let you know about your skirt being caught in your bag"
It is too long, the length makes it way too intrusive and i'm not even sure i'll make it sound understandable with my accent. I don't want my intentions to be mistaken.

"Hey darling, do like this" i could say by pointing her bag so she gets it quicker with the help of my body language. Perhaps it is too direct and patronising, it could sound misogynistic.

"Oh be careful, i think your bag is doing a trick on you" i could say as a joke with a funny tone.

She's gonna think i'm taking the piss.

I accelerate the pace to get near her, i think again and slow down to not be too close to her and go step towards the road. I raise my voice a bit.

"Hey man, your skirt" i
"Ah thanks" woman in skirt
"No worries" i

She lifts her handbag and pulls down her skirt without altering her face expression, as if it was almost point-less of me pointing it out to her, as if in a gentrified neighbourhood, we shouldn't show attention to peo-ple's embarrassment. Perhaps her eyebrows were say-ing something else, perhaps they were just irritated. I try not to go too deep in the interpretation of her reaction and cross the street to change pavement. I can't really be walking behind her anymore and i still don't want to hear the hasty cadence of her heels.

A guy is sitting on the floor with his dog, he is asking for some spare change, i reply i don't have any and i apol-ogise. Beggars often make me apologise even though i haven't done anything wrong. I'm wondering if he takes the chance to be seated to meditate sometimes.

A woman approaches with a leaflet in her hands, she talks to me loudly and asks me if i'd be interested in supporting a cause she seems to get support from. I apologise again even though i am not sorry.

I hear the sound of skateboards as i enter the square, sweaty guys are pushing and rolling. Happiness rushes through my veins to see that Holmes, Ollie and Kootch are there by the bench. Holmes is gesticulating, the conversation must be entertaining, i only get the last bit of what he is saying as i arrive, "Planet earth is an asylum, how can you base a logic on one eating another? It's mad, if you're on planet earth, you're a fucking lunatic". We slap hands, they mock me for not being sweaty and for carrying a cardigan on my arm, i appreciate the attention and the playful tone. Everyone looks like a new person under today's atmospheric conditions, i am rediscovering my friends. I sit next to them whilst other guys are trying to slide smoothly on the rail further down the square. The coolness of the activity, making a deck of wood take off from the floor just with a slap and a drag, just with the feet, it always captivates me.

High on wheels, on boards like pirates attacking curbs, rolling with balance and poise, they are floating over the concrete. Skateboarders are the surfers of urban landscapes, with the shimmer of the sea replaced by pieces of metal or glass on the floor. They flow and fall and fall and flow. It is about the steez, to kill the slow mo and to have the dignity of trying again when it hurts to fall. Someone manages a trick and everyone cheers, i'm wondering how circus acrobats would rate their prowess. A wooden deck, four wheels, a piece of grip, two trucks and ball bearings, the simplicity of the concept is impeccable. I wish i could do more than pushing and turning, although the satisfaction i get from watching is enough to keep me entertained. I like the noise of the skateboards popping, sliding, grinding, landing and rolling again. I like the urban games better than the olympic ones, because they seem accessible, less constipated and more fun. In here poetry is endless, city is the limit. These guys look at squares, benches, slopes, curbs and urban infrastructures with motion in their heads. It is all about movement against static. It is a type of love given to the town, a communion between humans and architecture that requires more than just balance. It takes a frame of mind that can cross barriers, that can push limits and that can go against the law. It is more than rolling, it is exercising freedom. It is a way to deal with gravity that preserves the mind. Just watching them doing their thing and my thoughts are rejuvenated.

"Have a go Brémond, you love skateboard but i never see you on one" Kootch
"I don't want to get sweaty, i told you, i'm on my way to work" i
"I don't mean today, seriously, you should skate with us, that'd be fun" Kootch
"That'd be fun for you, i don't have any perseverance to give to a wooden board with wheels, i'm really fine

with just watching" i

"Pervert" Kootch says as he pushes away to the next curb.

Watching them skating inspires me sometimes to do tricks in my head with letters, interpreting their acrobatics by drawing parallels with words, skate-wording. I let my mind drift away with the game.

Kootch likes doing simple tricks, going forward and backward the same way, like 'KAYAK', 'MADAM', 'SEX-ES', 'LEVEL', 'RADAR' or 'WOW'.

"Kootch is right, you should have a go, look, you could start with simple palindromes, they're not too difficult, once you know, it is pretty straight forward, look, that's 'STATS', a basic one, you should be able to do it, no trouble" Holmes suggests as he demonstrates the trick.

"You can go a little harder than that" Ollie adds, teasing Holmes by doing a 'NO LEMON' to 'NO MELON'. I wooh at him, expressing my appreciation.

Holmes is bending the knees, adjusting his stance, popping on the tail to make a classic 'STEP ON NO PETS' followed by a 'STACK CATS'. I wooh again louder.

On the other side of the square, Ollie fails on trying a 'CIGAR TOSS IT IN A CAN IT IS SO TRAGIC' which looks like quite a hard one to do.

The level is going higher, Kootch goes behind him and nails a 'LIVE ON NO EVIL'.

Ollie looks slightly annoyed since he's missed his trick and Kootch managed to do his with such ease. He gets back on his board to try out a harder combination and kills a 'NO CAB, NO TUNA NUT ON BACON'. A smile of satisfaction grows immediately on his face, every-one shouts, some of the skaters on the other side of the square are praising him by making noise with their board. Ollie's smile is getting slightly tainted with awkwardness. Ollie is quite competitive, in other words, he gets his motivation from trying to do better than others, so in a way, the people who skate with him should also be cred-ited for the success of his tricks. I'm trying to find a way to formulate this thought as a joke but i can't find a good angle so i keep it for myself. I wish i had filmed what he just did and could replay the whole action in a slower motion.

Holmes discreetly drops a 'SENILE FELINES' which looks quite stylish to me.

"Oh nice one! See, it is not about how complex the trick is, it's about the steez" Kootch
"Sure ting" i
"Brémond, why don't you try a 'SWAP PAWS', that'd be your style" Holmes
"Ok, give me that board, let see if can manage to do a 'POP' at least" i

"Go for it, do your own thing, just remember, there are two i's in 'imagine', it's important to keep them open" Holmes

"I've got the two i's of a musician, it should help" i

As a goofy, i put my right foot on the front side of the board and push with the left. I push for a moment and let myself roll just to get the feeling of being on a skateboard, sensing the balance of my body standing on the moving platform. I press on one side of the deck and it changes direction. I adjust the position of my front foot and start to feel more comfortable. I push again more confidently, i feel like trying a simple trick. I manage to get a 'PAN NAP' on the way like beginners do which is super easy. I am not sure i can get confident enough to try a 'SWAP PAWS' yet but i can feel the inspiration coming. An exciting idea pops into my mind. I'm thinking of an easy trick that could be fun to do. It is a maneuver that requires good equilibrium. I am going to try to stay on the same word and take letters off one by one without affecting the sound balance of the word. It is quite easy to do but somehow quite entertaining, it goes like 'QUEUE, QUEU, QUE, QU, Q'.

"What was that?! That's cool, keep the board, do some more!" Holmes

"Cheers, no i must stop, i don't want to sweat" i

"How would you not sweat anyway? Just sitting here makes me sweat" Holmes

"I've got to go to work and i've got a date afterwards" i

"You've got a date? Who's the bird?" Holmes

"I don't know her, i've never met her, i've found her on my phone, i mean, online, with an app" i

"Online dating, it's the commodification of the most precious thing ever!" Kootch

"Don't tell me you can't find a woman without an app" Holmes

"Well, i don't know, i wanted to try, d'you know what i mean?" i

"Is she hot? Show us a pic" Ollie

"It is hard to tell only with pictures, i think she's cute, she seems to have a good chat too" i

"As a basic rule, you don't want the woman to be too hot though, the hot ones are normally boring in bed, you want an average one who's going to bring some fire to the bedroom" Kootch

"Why's that?" Ollie

"Because hot girls are too used to getting everything they want, they rarely develop a sense of initiative in bed, they act like princesses" Kootch

"How would you know?" Ollie

"You knobhead" Kootch

"Personally, i like the ones who are sexy and funny and she seems to have the two, so why not?" i

"I'm pretty sure there are plenty of sexy and funny birds around the corner, how come you haven't spotted one already, how come you need a phone for that? You're French for fucksake!" Holmes

"I don't know, maybe it is like a hide-and-seek game and i still haven't found her. Actually, i need to go, what are you guys doing later?" i

"There's a party on Alexander's boat tonight" Holmes

"Really? Oh that's a shame, i'm going to miss that" i

"What are you talking about? Your night sounds pretty exciting" Holmes

"Well, i don't know about that, we'll see when i'm there" i
My phone is ringing, Kootch is checking his as he's got the same ringtone.

"Oh man! It's Jeanne... A Parisian bird, how come is she calling me now? Man, she is quite a number, you would love her, why the f is she calling me now for?" i

"Jeanne of Arc?" Kootch

"We haven't been communicating in years, why is she calling me?" i

"Pick up the call you bell end!" Kootch

"That's unusual..." i

"Come on, answer the phone!" Kootch

"Allo?" i

[street noise]

"Allo, allo?" i

[cars noise]

"Allo oui bonjour?" i

[walking noise]

I look at Kootch, he is expecting me to start a conversation in French, i realise i shouldn't have promoted it.

"She is pocket-calling me" i

I hung up. The boys laugh.

I have not thought of Jeanne in ages, most guys find her very attractive but i don't think she is my type, i am not sure about her sense of humour. Weirdly enough, her pocket-calling me almost makes me feel like it is a bad joke from her.

Let's text Amy, let's confirm the place and time for later.

There's already a few people sitting around the tables outside on the terrace. It is a small and cute old pub located on the corner of a backstreet of the neighbourhood of Angel. It has green facade and green plants on its windowsills. It is called by the name of the British essayist and poet, Charles Lamb, who wrote "My theory is to enjoy life, but the practice is against it.". I like to see people coming here, demonstrating their interpretation of that quote. On the pavement, the A-board has been redesigned. Hugh must have done this one, he usually draws funny lamb characters with puns around the word 'lamb'. Today, there is a lamb drawn in a prison cell with 'the silence of the lamb' written at the bottom, there used to be a lamb by a Lamborghini, i quite liked inspector Colambo too. There are two little olive trees by one of the two entrances, i touch their leaves to say hi as i enter.

It is quiet inside, the ceiling fans are spinning full blast, Richard is greeting me from behind the bar with contagious positive energy, i reply with similar enthusiasm. The joie de vivre of this Welshman is always inspiring, it

almost doesn't feel like working with the kind of manager he is and i blame his insatiable taste and passion
for food and drinks for the extra kilos i put on recently.
The wooden floor is creaking hello as i step on it to go
hook my cardigan on the small coat hanger by the kitch-
en. There are only Yuki's bag and top here, summer has
dried out the rack. Yuki is from Japan, he's been living in
the UK longer than me, i think he is a great chef and so
do the customers. He is also partly responsible for the
expansion of my belly.

In the kitchen on his side today, there is George, an English commis-chef. Both of them are musicians, both of
them are into Rock music, both of them have their own
musical projects but they play together sometimes. I
reach the sink to wash my hands, the temperature in
the kitchen is way hotter than usual despite the two big
metallic fans blowing air from opposite sides of the room.
Their radio is blasting off Led Zeppelin's riffs.

 "Bonjour!" i
 "Bonjour mon ami, comment ça va?" Yuki
 "Feeling good man, how are you guys doing? Are you
  coping with the summer heat? It is even hotter in here
  than outside" i
 "The extractor fan broke, it's hell in here" Yuki
 "Yeah hell, hell yeah" George
 "The extractor fan broke? Oh shit, how?" i
 "It just stopped working" George
 "So the menu will be restricted because we can't use
  the grill until it is fixed, we can only do cold dishes

tonight" Yuki

"But it is inhuman working in these conditions" i

"There's nothing we can do, it's completely fucked"
George

"It's going to take a week to fix it they say" Yuki

"We'll be dead by then" George

"Oh man that's crazy" i

"What can we do? The company doesn't want to close the
kitchen, it is not a good enough reason apparently" Yuki

"Have you guys got drinks? Can i bring some sort of
cold beverages?" i

"It's ok thanks, we've got this bucket of iced water" George

"You guys should drink hot tea instead" i

"What?" George

"Yeah seriously, that's what some people do in the South
of France, by drinking something warm, your body adapts
to the hot temperature better and you sweat less" i

"There's no way i drink hot tea with this heat" Yuki

I leave the heat and go to the bar, lowering my head
enough so it doesn't hit the shelf above the entry, i hug
Richard. Rich is a musician too, music never leaves him,
it shows off naturally when the pub doesn't require too
much of his attention. When he's got a free hand, Rich
hits rhythms on any surfaces that can give an interesting
sound. If a pen, a knife or a kitchen tool leans around,
there are good chances that he will pick it up to throw
patterns on a glass, a beer mat or on an ice bucket.

Jack has just arrived, it must be the first time that i've
seen him without a hat on. Jack lives round the corner,

he comes here every day. Jack has been into fashion all his life, the hat he normally wears is similar to the one Pharrell Williams has brought back on trend some time ago. Jack says it is Pharrell who has copied him and that it is not the first time Pharrell has done it. He also says that since Pharrell wears it, people compliment him on the street whereas before he would get funny looks for wearing such a hat and so it is a good thing Pharrell made it popular in a way. Jack is much older than Pharrell but it would be hard for anyone to give him an age. His attitude to life, his skin tone and his stylish way of dressing would make it almost impossible to guess he was born in the 60's. Jack says he is the one who introduced London to Jean Paul Gaultier and Jean Paul Gaultier to London. Jack is not married anymore and has no children, he comes here to drink everyday but a very small amount. He only drinks halves of the lightest lager we have on draft. He likes to sit on the right end of the bar and often requires, as a joke, to have his name on the stool so nobody takes it when he is not using it. Usually, the locals gravitate around his spot as he is mates with all of them. I don't know about the influence he has on fashion these days but he certainly made this side of the bar the fashionable side.

We serve ales, flat ones and other ones with bubbles. We serve some at room temperature and others that are colder. We don't serve mainstream ones, Rich's standards wouldn't allow that. The radio that is playing on the speakers is French and it has nothing to do with me. I actually didn't know that station before i started working here. A previous owner of the pub was French and some French touches remain on the walls, like the French maps and designs of old French spirit posters, however, they have nothing to do with the radio's selection. It is Rich's choice to play it. In fact, it is not entirely down to him we have this French radio on. It is down to Jack who made him discover it a while ago. I don't know the person who Jack gots it from but to most customers, when they hear the French talking in between songs, it makes no doubt to them that the radio choice is mine. It is called 'fip radio' and they play an excellent and random selection of music. They could play Opera music just after a track by Bob Marley. They are quite playful with the music, sometimes they only play songs with lyrics that relate to a chosen theme or play different covers of the same song in a row and they don't have any adverts. It is clearly my favourite radio on the planet at the moment, they are currently playing 'Guitar Makossa' by Francis Bebey.

Rich is pouring a glass of chilled Pinot noir, some like their red wine cold, it is rather unusual but it kind of makes sense on a day like this. I go shake Jack's hand with the intention to do it differently than i would normally do, just for the sake of changing or perhaps as a reaction to seeing him without a hat which somehow gives him a different attitude. As the man's got a taste for the street culture, i let myself improvise a style that requires twists, slides and hooking each other's fingers.

Jack follows the whole move naturally, instinctively and without questioning it, like he already knew the choreography. I grab a half pint glass and pour his favourite lager in it.

"Hello darling how are you?" Jack

"Hey Jack how are you? Where's your hat?" i

"It is too hot for a hat today darling, would you mind keeping my bag behind the bar while i go to the toilet please?" Jack

"Sure, what about a straw hat? I'm sure you could pull a straw hat off" i

"I've got a few of those yeah, but they are all at my ex's house, she's still got so much of my stuff" Jack

I place the full half on the bar and get to the till to enter Jack's drink on his monthly tab. Jack drinks everyday but only pays once a month, the man knows how to balance out the pleasures. Rich comes beside me and waits for his turn.

"Guess who came earlier?" Rich

"Oh, was it a lady?" i

"Indeed, she came again" Rich

"The Scottish one?" i

"Yes indeed" Rich

"Really? Isn't it the third time she comes here in a week or so? She must have a thing for the Welshness" i

"She was in a short dress, she looked quite sexy, i think i've been charmed" Rich

"That's good news" i

Rich is generally quite fussy with the ladies, not necessarily about their looks but about their manners. He often says a little detail can destroy all the charm of a woman, he says that he prefers them a bit wild, that he is looking for passion and magic. I have only briefly met the Scottish girl twice and i can't really tell if she matches his expectations but it feels good to feel a bit of action surrounding me, it stimulates the atoms of love in the air.

Gerry and Lorraine have just come in, walking slowly, greeting everyone with a soft voice and an affectionate smile like they always do. Lorraine sits down on one of the couches, Gerry comes to the bar and orders a round for him and his long time partner. She usually takes a Pinot Noir, at room temperature, he likes a German Pilsner in a big glass with a big handle. This beer requires more attention than others when being poured, it creates way too much foam. We don't know if the problem is coming from the keg, the line, the pressure or the nozzle, the white froth is coming out in abundance so we have to tilt the glass with dexterity and let it overflow whilst keeping the tap running filling up the pint. Fortunately the glass is designed so there's room for the foam, German style, there is a little line to set a limit to half litre, after that line it is where the cloud sits. Gerry is going to have his seventy ninth birthday soon, which he wouldn't celebrate if it was a round number he mentioned the other day. He says he just wants partying on the odd ones. Gerry likes to say that with the life he's had, he always believed that he would pass away at the age of sixty years old, so since he's passed sixty, it is all bonus. He also says that his sixty ninth birthday was his favourite because the number reminds him of a scene that happened to him during a summer in France when he was younger but he would never talk about it in the presence of Lorraine.

Gerry and Lorraine were both adopted when they were children, and maybe because they had to find their marks without knowing who their real parents were or because of their age, or because of the beautiful light in their eyes and their pleasant sympathy, i always try my best to make them feel good. They met each other at the age of sixty and have stayed as a couple ever since, enjoying the quieter moments of life together. Gerry is a good looking man who still goes to the gym a few days a week. Lorraine is pretty too, she used to be an athlete, she used to swim at a high level, competing in the European championships.

"Can i have one of those and one of those please?" Gerry
"Certainly sir, let me take a wild guess, could it be a Pinot Noir and one of those Pilsner sir?" i
"It wasn't too wild for a guess was it?" Gerry
"I had good clues, how are you? How's the weather treating you today?" i
"Well, it reminds me of my time in your part of the world when i was living in the South of France" Gerry

"Oh come on Gerry, surely it must have been hotter than today, right?" i

"Well, you're right it was hotter, but i was handling it better when i was your age, so when you think about it, it feels about the same to me now to what it was back then" Gerry

"That is a fair point" i

I push the handle back, a bit of the golden liquid has overflown on my hand and on my shoe. I sort out the wine and pick the tenner off Gerry's hand, i cash the two drinks and bring him back the change. A woman enters the bar from the other side, she is wearing a top with a low cleavage that reveals she is not wearing a bra. She orders a Gin with slimline Tonic. I rarely look at big breasts, i like looking at derrieres better, but i find it kind of difficult looking at her in the eyes when there are obvious nipples pointing in my direction. I grab a little bottle of slimline Tonic and pop the lid off. The 'pshitt' sound that it makes is quite satisfying to my ears, it evokes an exotic freshness somehow. I take a small glass with my other hand and put both of them near the ice bucket. It seems the heat has been making the ice cubes sweat and i can't manage to find decent shapes of cubes to structure the drink. They're all too small. I apologise to the woman without looking at her breasts and inform Rich that i am going downstairs to get some more ice whilst emptying the bucket of slushed cubes into the sink under the coffee machine. I leave the bar and walk through the corridor by the kitchen to the cellar door, i open it and walk down the steep staircase holding the cold container against my belly. The ceiling of the cellar is so low that i need to slightly curve my back and neck to avoid knocking my head against the old wooden beams. They look so old, they look like they could collapse anytime soon but i've been told they mustn't be judged by their appearances and that they should be fine for many more decades. I turn left to the ice machine by the washing machine. The machines stand there side by side, one makes water spin, the other one shapes water into six-sided solids. I scoop enough of the cubes so my bucket looks full, under the cellar light, they are shining like precious stones from underground. The staircase is creaking as i am climbing it back up, the wooden door makes another vintage noise of the same kind. I carefully push it, slowly, in case a woman, rushed by the amount of drink in her bladder, is pacing her way to the toilet, as the door blocks access to it when it's opened. I can't hear anyone so i continue my way up and reach the surface. Back through the corridor, Led Zeppelin is still playing in the kitchen, perhaps the playlist will lay down 'Stairway To Heaven' soon so the cooks can find an exit from hell.

I put the ice bucket back to its spot, scoop out three brand new cubes and throw them in the short glass. I pinch a wedge of lime and abandon it on the cubes after a little squeeze. I grab one of the green bottles of Gin, unscrew the lid and fill up a measure of 25cl above the glass to pour it inside. I take the little bottle of mixer and empty it onto the spirit, pieces of ice and fruit. It goes like an ocean wave breaking on some rocks. The fizzy reaction makes the drink look more exciting, bubbles are popping around the icebergs and the floating bits of green pulp. I grab two little black straws and place them in a way so they remain straight up to the side like antennas. The lazy tubes tend to go horizontal if not stuck by the cubes. The radio is playing a song that i have never heard before, the rhythm goes in triplets and Rich already started tapping the beat on a beer tap handle. If Donal was working today, i bet he would be playing to that song too, adding some staccatos with a pen to the mix, which would inevitably lead me to make a sound too. I bring the glass to the bar for the lady and present the card machine so she can tap it with her contactless card. She thanks me, i smile back, avoiding reflecting her boobsy language with my eyes. She turns back and almost naturally, i check out how her bum looks, just to figure out the combo i suppose. Her back side is not dressed to show off as much. I go put the card machine back on its base and close the deal on the till.

There are tiny flies flying behind the bar, we could do without them but it is the sugar that attracts them. It also attracts ants and we could do without them too but sugar attracts customers and we couldn't do without them.

Spirit bottles surround the bar like trophies, like bar ornaments on the shelves. The Whiskeys are placed strategically, going from very smokey to less smokey. They're from Scotland, Ireland and from Japan. We have only one bottle of Cognac, people call it brandy though.

There are hops with branches attached to the ceiling above the bar for decoration and to remind people where most beers come from. There are two fridges with glass windows, the one on the left holds white wines, rosé, Prosecco, Champagne and a bottle of Pinot Noir. The one on the right displays beer bottles made locally, from Belgium or from Germany. I'm not sure if Rich did it consciously but the fridge on the left is mostly requested by women and the one on the right by men, which gives to these two identical fridges kind of a different gender.

I see Ed on the other side of the bar waving at me for his second cider, his usual that he's paid for already. Ed generally orders one cider, pays for two and shows a hand when the first one is finished and can be refilled. Ed would never ask for a new glass, he wants both in the in same pint glass, one after another obviously. Ed rarely talks much, he always comes here with earplug headphones in his ears. It makes him look like a security guard, reading the free newspaper, looking like he is connected to something that has nothing to do with us. Sometimes, he takes one earplug off to engage a conversation but unfortunately it is quite hard for me to exchange with him as he is a bit deaf and doesn't always get my accent. My pronunciation is definitely not great but his asks for more than just attention, many of us don't quite get him. Ed doesn't have all his teeth nor a very expressive body language which don't really help for the fluidity of the communication. Nonetheless, there is a gentle light in his eyes, there is something nice about Ed that makes me want to know him better, even though it is quite impossible for me from that side of the bar. The best i can do is to make him understand that i am aware of his habits, that he doesn't need to mention to me that he's paid for the cider already so he can stay in his comfort zone between the lines of his newspaper and his music or whatever he is listening to.

The glasswasher needs emptying, its red light has turned green. I open the door and the hot steam rushes out of it in a hurry, getting out of the machine as if it was chased by something. The glasses are so hot, it feels like they would cook my fingertips if i held them for too long. I place them on the shelf straight away without waiting for them to dry out like i used to do when i started the job, like i was advised to during my training. I guess i've built up enough confidence to assess when i can allow myself such extravagance.

George comes out of the kitchen and puts a plate of pasta at the rear of the bar by the dining room, "Staff food's ready!" he says and goes back into the furnace. Rich is not hungry and invites me to go for it. Staff food is often pasta, "Staff food should never be special" some chefs say in this business, but pasta made by Yuki can be special. Today, the spaghetti are covered with homemade pesto and olive oil and they are at their full length, not broken into small pieces like some people do, which give me a bit of foreplay rolling them around the fork before eating them.

Today i'm eating on my own, the number of staff is reduced during the summer, as is the number of customers. There is no one in the dining room, it feels so different without heads, maybe that's the way it is on Saturday afternoons. I'm sitting on a tall stool, spinning a fork into spaghetti until the length gets more convenient for the mouth. A new notification just appeared on my phone, i look at it trying not to get involved with it too much so i can appreciate the food better. It is my date. The message is a reply to my earlier text so there is no point in writing again until we meet. The phone is trying to get my attention, to make me scroll into feeds, to make me forget about what i am currently doing. I am re-focussing on the delicious pasta, re-acknowledging the fineness of the taste, reminding myself they've been made by a great chef. I put the phone down with the screen facing the table and keep on rolling, it feels better than scrolling, i'm trying not to think about the date.

Some of the usual crew has arrived around Jack, i can see Nick, Ryan and Oscar, perhaps Eddie will come later. Rich is taking care of them, i bring my plate to the kitchen and go collect the empty glasses left around the pub.

  "Thanks for the pesto pasta Yukisan, that was delicious" i
  "You should drink Pastis now, so it will be pasta, pesto, Pastis" Yuki
  "I like Pastis, but Pastis is usually before the meal, it is a drink you have as an apéritif, not as a digestive" i
  "I know" Yuki
  "Have a pistachio pastry for dessert then!" George

I head back out. If i was quick enough, i could have continued the joke with something about a 'pastiche' but it didn't find me in time, it is 'l'esprit d'escalier' we say in French. I've eaten too much, i need to undo my belly button.

Picking up glasses is a bit like picking up flowers but

with less bending action. It doesn't require much ability, just being able to assess when the glasses are empty, to pay attention to those that contain spirits without mixers, as the glasses can still hold a small layer of the beverage, a precious last sip. Picking up glasses also requires balance when piling them up and carrying them amongst unpredictable drunk people. Apart from that, it is fairly easy, although it is like anything, it is harder after eating too much pasta.

I go check the outside, the sun is still hitting generously, the awning is down but the shadow it creates is not big enough to shield both olive trees. The green of some of their leaves is turning a bit yellow, as if some blue had evaporated into the blue sky. On the way back, i stop by Gerry and Lorraine's table, the blue of his eyes is vibrant, present and pleasant like the sea on a sunny day.

"Hi Lorraine how's things? Have you guys been to the gym today?" i
"Oh no, i don't go to the gym, only Gerry goes" Lorraine
"I didn't go today, but i've been twice this week" Gerry
"I thought you guys were training together, i thought you were following Lorraine's butterfly swimming techniques to broaden your shoulders" i
"I can't do the butterfly, i maybe could do the caterpillar but not the butterfly, you know Lorraine was a pro" Gerry
"I know yeah, the butterfly is so hard, so exhausting, i can't do it too" i

"No, it's not, it is actually the easiest once you know the technique" Lorraine

"Well, i don't think i am built for it Lorraine" i

"But you can play instruments, playing an instrument is great" Gerry

"It can be fun" i

"I'm going to tell you something" Gerry

"What is it?" i

"You see, i have three big regrets in life, one is that i haven't learned to speak any other languages properly and two is that i never learned to play an instrument, and you, you have two of the three!" Gerry

"What is the third one?" i

"If only i could remember it..." Gerry says as he raises his pint to his mouth, we laugh and i go back to work.

A group of five people enter the bar and sit by the table on the corner. The atmosphere is building up, one of them goes ordering to Rich, i go back to the dishwasher to unload my fragile pile and to salute the boys around Jack, i shake their hands in a formal way.

I write down 'Sausage Roll / bar / Ryan' on the notepad, tear the page off, take it to the kitchen and clip the paper on the silver rail above the fan where orders are usually queuing. Yuki and George are in the middle of a conversation about noodles.

"Noodles? Are you going to put noodles on the menu Yuki?" i

"No way, i was only telling George about the corner shop near my house" Yuki

"What's up with it?" i

"They keep bags of noodles on a top shelf and because i'm not that tall, it's difficult for me to reach them, and if you think about it, it's mostly Asian people who eat noodles and most Asian people are small, so it is stupid keeping them on a high shelf" Yuki

"That is a point, i've never thought about it this way" i

"Yeah, because bread and cheese are always easy to reach" George

"Did you tell them to change it?" i

"Indeed i did" Yuki

"Did you?" George

"Well yeah, if you live in London and don't learn about cultural differences, there is no point living in London, of course i told the guy" Yuki

"That's fair enough, bro, what's on the ticket?" George

"A sausage roll, it is for Ryan so no ketchup on the side please, otherwise he is going to be upset" i

"Upset? But what's wrong with ketchup?" George

"Ryan has a phobia about ketchup, maybe he got attacked by a ketchup jar when he was young" Yuki

"What? A ketchup phobia? That's crazy, that must be awful, ketchup is everywhere" George

"No it's not, i never eat ketchup" i

"Really? Never?" George

"Yep, never, it is too close to a smoothie for me to use it with fries or whatever people use it with" i

"Is Ketchup not popular in France?" Yuki

"I'm not really sure, obviously you can find ketchup everywhere so i'd say it must be popular but it's like McDonalds, they're everywhere but i never eat there, so i wouldn't know how busy they are" i

"I never eat at McDonalds either" Yuki

"Everyone says that but still, they are everywhere" i

"Listen to that, my uncle from Italy told me a story the other day, he said that in a small town in Tuscany, a guy opened a burger joint next to a Mcdonalds and apparently, after a few months, the McDonalds had to close down because the guy took over the whole burger business" George

"Really? That's amazing!" Yuki

"They know their food in Italy" i

"They certainly do" George

Back to the bar, Ryan and Jack call for my attention but not like the way they do when they need a drink, something else is going on. Oscar and Nick, who are sitting on the stools behind them, know what's cooking, they're boosting my curiosity with their smile. I get closer to them and lean my head over like i was going to listen to a secret. Jack leans towards my ear and talks quietly, he discreetly points to a woman who is sitting with the group of people that just arrived at the table in the corner.

"Do you remember the name of the French actress who was in that late 80's movie? She looks like the girl over there" Jack

"French actress? Really? She doesn't necessarily look French to me" i

"Yes she does, look at her hair" Ryan

"What? Just because she's got dark hair, doesn't mean she's French" i

"I bet you she's French, look at the way she holds her head, just like the actress i'm telling you about, oh come on, what's the name of that actress? Jack

"I'm not sure who she could look like really, what's the movie called?" i

"I can't remember it either, but the title is the name of the character of that actress in the movie" Jack

"What? Amélie?" i

"No, not Audrey Tautou, it's a movie from the late 80's" Jack

"Late 80's..." i

"You know that scene, she gets mad and throws everything through the window" Jack

"Typical French woman" Oscar

"I'm sure you know that scene, they live by a beach, the first scene of the movie is a sex scene" Jack

"Oh i know who you mean, i can't see much resemblance though, you're talking about Betty Blue aren't you? The name of the actress is Beatrice Dalle" i

"Betty Blue! That's the one!" Jack

"Come on, she doesn't look like Beatrice Dalle at all, she's probably Italian or Spanish, you guys just fantasise about French women too much that you see them everywhere" i

"I fucking love French ladies, they're classy and naughty, both at the same time" Jack

"They've got that je ne sais quoi" Ryan

"You guys don't know what you're talking about, i was with a French girl for one year, it ended two years ago and i still haven't totally recovered" Oscar

"What?" Ryan

"Ask Rich what he thinks about French women, Rich tell them" Oscar

"My ex-girlfriend is French, it ended a year and a half ago and i'm still heartbroken" Rich

"French pattern" i

"They're cruel, you give them your heart and they throw it on the floor and stamp on it, they crush it to pieces, they're horrible" Oscar

"They're like drugs, the most vicious kinds of drugs, they play their tricks on you until you love them and once you've given them everything you've got, they leave you with nothing" Rich

"You guys sound a bit dramatic, i know some very nice French women" Jack

"Interesting to hear, i'd say French women have a special demeanor and it depends on how you behave with them, with some of them you have to know the trick" i

"What trick?" Oscar

"You need to know how to deal with the French whim" i

"What do you mean?" Rich

"Well, when your French woman uses the whimsical tone regularly when asking you for things, you have to be aware of it and kind of refuse to give her whatever it is she wants from you" i

"But that's just rude" Oscar

"No, that's not always rude, that's self defense, because if you respond positively to whimsical requests too often, the less interest she will have for you, however nice you think you are. I know it is a warm feeling to please someone but you have to do it carefully as that's usually where the trouble starts" i

"You French people are just rude in general that's all it is" Oscar

"I dated a French woman a long time ago, she's always been nice to me" Jack

"How did it end?" Oscar

"She wanted to travel and i didn't, that's all" Jack

"Was she a hippy?" Ryan

"No she wasn't, she had high standards actually, but she moved to New York and i stayed in London, simple as that" Jack

"Never again, not for me" Oscar

"I wouldn't mind mingling with this one" Ryan

"I don't think she's French" i

"She'll do, i'll play some Serge Gainsbourg in the bedroom with a nice bottle of wine or some French Champagne, croissants for breakfast, that should do it" Ryan

"She is French" Jack

"Have you heard her talking yet or not?" i

"Nah, her friend ordered the drinks" Jack

"I'd say she's French" Oscar

"Hard to tell, to be honest she reminds me of a friend of mine from Greece" Nick

"Will we make a bet? Go to her and say something in French, we'll see how she reacts" Ryan

"Just call her Betty Blue and see what she says" Jack
"Let's bet, five quid, or the next round" Ryan
"No need to bet, she's French i guarantee you" Jack
"It's my round anyway, same again please and one for
 yourself" Ryan

I thank him and decline the offer. The food i had was
rather heavy and digestion is taking most of my energy. It wouldn't be fair to give my body any more work to
do. I already have to be standing and to be available to
customers when i wish i could be seated. I prepare half
a lager for Jack, a pint of lager for Nick, a pint of stout
for Oscar and a vodka lime and soda for Ryan. The bell
is ringing from the kitchen, that must be Ryan's sausage
roll.

As i go to get the food, Rich makes me notice the couple
he just served that went to sit in the hidden corner. He
reckons they must be on their first date judging by the
way they ordered their drinks. The hidden corner is only
visible from inside the bar and quite often couples go
there to get some intimacy. We find it funny the way first
dates tend to evolve sometimes, they are usually very
well behaved and overpolite until they start kissing. As
soon as their lips meet each other, they lose their inhi-
bitions and forget about the world around them. In London, public display of affection is not as tolerated as it is
in Paris. Nobody wants to observe the art of kissing here,
lovers should hide, same with music, no obvious saucy
business allowed. When The Beatles wanted to express a

strong sexual desire in a song, they would write a chorus like 'I want to hold your hand' to keep it UK radio-friendly. Serge Gainsbourg never had these types of problems with self-censorship in France. If he had sang lyrics like 'I want to hold your hand', people would have assumed he was singing about some sort of perverse hand-fetish. Anyway, cultural differences are interesting, although in a pub, alcohol dissipates those differences. Alcohol is international, it doesn't care about the codes of the countries of origin, it connects people regardless, it makes it obvious that humans are not so far from animals. Sometimes around those tables, magic happens and it is quite surprising to see how some people can change after just few glasses of alcoholic potions. Some of them need alcohol to open themselves and to reveal how shiny they are on the inside, a bit like bags of crisps, and sometimes, it is a wonderful thing to witness.

The sausage roll looks like it is ready to feed somebody. I grab the plate, a fork, a knife, a napkin and deliver them on the bar next to Ryan. The cute brunette stands up, the one who is presumed to be French. She walks around the table where her friends are sitting and continues towards the toilets, i'd bet she is French now i've seen the way she moves. Ryan is staring at her derrière, i look at it too. It looks so peachy in these jeans that it is hard not to look at it parading across the room. Ryan looks back at me like i had done a crime, he is pulling down his eyebrows, tilting his head like he is willing to tell me off. Discreetly, we smile at each other, i whisper to him, "She could be French actually..." and keep on smiling.

We don't only serve drinks and food behind the bar, we also refill people's phone batteries. These ones are easier to top up, they never overflow, although they can start ringing. It's funny how quick i can be inspired to judge someone just by hearing the melody of their ringtone sometimes.

The woman comes back from the toilet, she reaches the bar and asks me for a glass of tap water with a strong French accent, making sound the letter 'r' of 'water' very similarly to the way i do. Jack was right, she is definitely French, i contain my reaction, i can feel his smirk from his corner.

"Hi, can i have a glass of tap water please?" French woman
"Certainly, would you like ice with your water?" i
"Euh excuse me?" French woman
"Any ice with the water?" i
"Are you serious?" French woman
"What do you mean?" i
"Seriously? Are you mocking my accent?" French woman
"What? No, absolutely not, why would i do such a thing?" i
"Stop imitating my accent then, it is really rude" French woman
"I am not imitating your accent at all, and sorry if my accent is reminding you of yours but i am French myself" i

"Ha really? Hahaha! You have such a strong accent!"
French woman

"I know, i've tried to improve it but it just doesn't work,
i've given up a long time ago" i

"Haha! That's quite funny, you sound English when
you say 'i know' even though you have such a strong
French accent, it is a bit ridiculous" French woman

"Well, London is the city where i've lived the longest, so
i suppose it makes sense to me if i get some nuances
here and there" i

"Haha 'i suppose', fuck! You're fucked man!" French
woman

"Now it is you mocking my accent" i

"Yeah, sorry it is too funny" French woman

"It is all a mess, when i speak in French in France, people rarely believe i'm French, they think i'm Canadian
or English or even from Belgique" i

"Go on, speak to me in French" French woman

"Would you like a slice of lemon too?" i

"Oui, s'il te plait" French woman

"Ok" i

"Allez! Parle moi en français" French woman

"No way, there's too much build up now, it wouldn't
make me sound natural, i'd fake it" i

"Allez, vas-y, come on" French woman

"No, no, no way, you're starting to make me feel shy now" i

"T'es pas drôle" French woman

"Sometimes i am, here, your water darling" i

"Darling, the way you say 'darling' is ridiculous, you
couldn't sound more French in your British way, oh

come on! Parle français, it is not very polite not reply-
ing in French to someone who talks to you in French
when you are a French person" French woman

"I tell you what is not polite, what is not polite is not
saying thank you when someone gives you a glass of
water" i

"Oh i'm so sorry sir, thank you kindly, you're such a
gentleman" French woman

"Oh, mais avec plaisir mademoiselle, tout le plaisir est
pour moi" i

"T'as dit deux fois 'plaisir', tu sonnes un peu redondant
en français en fait" French woman

"C'est parce que je fais une fixation dessus, si on doit
répéter un mot, autant que ce soit le 'plaisir' non?" i

"Fair enough, en fait c'est vrai, ton accent sonne un peu
bizarre" French woman

"Ah tu vois, i told you" i

"C'est cute, i think you should keep it" French woman

She goes back to her friends at the table with her glass
of iced water, Jack is enjoying his victory with all his face.
Ryan is calling for my attention, he wants me to lean my
head closer to him in order to have another discreet conversation, which i believe, considering that i just talked
with her, would make look too obvious that we're talking
about her. So because i refuse to lean, he tells me what
he wants to say by whispering. I understand at this point
that he's already had a few drinks elsewhere before coming here.

"Hey, don't steal my new girlfriend" Ryan

"What do you mean?" i

"The French girl, you guys were talking for a while, i noticed her first" Ryan

"Are you saying that you think she fancies me?" i

"I mean you guys have your French ways, you could keep me in the loop" Ryan

"Do you want me to introduce you to her? Is that what you mean?" i

"Well, that's what a friend would do, you're my friend right?" Ryan

"Ryan..." i

"I just ask, if you are my friend, are you my friend?" Ryan

"If she comes back here, i'll introduce her to you Ryan, i don't even know her name but i'll introduce you" i

"Come here, give me a hug" Ryan

"Ryan, please don't start, i am not going to give you a hug, please, let's try not to be too needy tonight, look i'm sweaty, it is embarrassing" i

Rich is bringing food to the first date table. It is quite unusual to see people having food on a first date, maybe they are not on their first date after all. The guy is salting his plate even though he hasn't yet tasted the food. Perhaps people who salt their plate before tasting the food must have an incredible sense of smell and can assess just by the odour the amount of salt missing.

I overhear Jack saying that he is not a sugar daddy, that

he is a Sweetex daddy.

Kev and Shirley are sitting by a table in the dinner area, i didn't notice them coming in. They already have drinks, their usual Pilsner and wheat beer. I realise i have forgotten again to bring them a signed copy of my record like i promised some time ago. They never miss a chance to remind me every time they see me and still, i keep on forgetting. When i offered the vinyl of my first EP to Gerry, it created some envious reactions and it is rather flattering to see people asking for my music, even if they ask to have it for free. Although there is an aspect about their request that makes me wonder. Kev and Shirley are deaf. I learnt ways to interact with them when they order drinks or when they are in the mood for expressing their thoughts. Sign language is actually quite convenient when the pub is crowded as we can communicate from afar and amongst noises, but i don't know how they could appreciate my songs. I have never given my music to people who can't hear, perhaps they are not completely deaf, perhaps they only hear what they want to hear, perhaps the record is for their children, i haven't yet dared to ask. The couple seems preoccupied today, they are moving their arms and faces more frantically than usual, i shall leave them alone.

There is laughter and good mood floating around the table where the French woman is sitting, positivity is attractive. I can't hear their conversation from behind the bar but i assume from the face she is pulling that her friend must be telling her something unusual. Her friend is prepping her hair, giving it some volume, i don't know if i fancy any of them but i know i miss a bit of romance in my life. She is pretty, she has noticed i'am gazing in her direction but i am not looking at her, i am just observing the distance that separates me from love.

"Stop looking at her" Ryan

"Sorry what?" i

"Stop looking at the French girl, you're gonna attract her attention too much and i want to make a move soon" Ryan

"I am not looking at her, i am just observing how far i am from love" i

"Oh you French poet" Ryan

Rich is smoking a cigarette outside, fip radio is playing 'Swinging On A Star' by Bing Crosby. I am squeezing half a lemon into a pint glass near the sink. Ed is leaving, he waves goodbye saying something i don't quite understand, i guess something funny telling by the tone. I smile at him and appreciate the energy the joke has brought to his eyes. It takes less time to fill up a pint glass with water than it takes with beer, the alcohol slows down everything i guess. I step back, turn my back to the audience and take a big gulp of lemon zesty water. The feeling that drinking it creates is so refreshing, if i had to describe it by using synesthesia, i would say it is similar to the freshness of a chorus by The Beach Boys. I feel the presence of someone staring at me by the bar. The customer can wait, i am pretending i haven't noticed them so i can have another gulp of good vibrations. I'm hiding behind my back. I can tell the person is looking in my direction, i can feel the weight of the look, i take another good swig and put the glass down to its bottom. I turn and face the person. It is a man, a man with dark hair, piercing blue eyes and a Rock n' Roll vibe all over him.

He is standing strong on his feet, not moving, staring at me, not saying a word like tough cowboys do in Western movies. He keeps on staring at me with his piercing eyes, i challenge his eye contact without saying a word either, standing still, we are watching each other, like cowboys do in duel in Spaghetti Western movies, not smiling, trying to keep a straight look. We're playing the comedy until we burst into laughters.

"My man, how are ya!?" Jimmy

"Amazing, look who's in da place!" i

"Good to see you my man!" Jimmy

"I could feel someone was looking at me and i was like, fuck it, i'll pretend i haven't seen, i am too thirsty, this person can wait" i

"I know, i was watching ya, taking your time, i was wondering how long it would take for you to look at me you snobby Frenchman" Jimmy

"Ah sorry bro, i was thirsty" i

"I don't blame ya, have you seen the weather? Amazing!" Jimmy

"Yeah, that's crazy, finally summer right? So where have you been? I haven't seen you in ages, have you been touring?" i

"Yeah man, just come back from Italy, it was great man, we had such a good time" Jimmy

"Oh man, let me say hello to you properly" i

I walk around the bar to hug the man who's back from tour. There are some hellos that need to be said with capital letters. Jimmy's band is called The Graveltones, they play a kind of heavy Blues Rock music. The energy they give on stage is mindblowing, they're a two piece band but they make a sound that easily equals the noise that double the amount of musicians would make. I return behind the bar. Jimmy tells me about the tour in Italy, how the food was tastebud-blowing and how he connected with a dog and he brought it back to London with him in the tour van. We keep the conversation going whilst i am pouring glasses to customers, juggling with the till, ice cubes, dishwasher, food orders or jug of ice water for the kitchen. Jimmy keeps on telling me about Italy, he says i should go on tour with them, i tell him i quite like the idea, thinking i could take the chance to write a book about being on the road with them, trying to capture their incredible energy with words. I tell him if a dog has been able to tour with them, i don't see why a cat couldn't. A friend of his enters the bar and i pour two more pints, they go outside to enjoy the sunshine and i keep on juggling with my responsibilities, apologising about the restricted food menu, collecting empty glasses and plates, slicing more bread, giving the attention that some customers require, avoiding splashing my face when changing kegs downstairs, checking the name of songs from the radio station, feeding phones with battery, emptying the bin behind the bar, asking people to stay on one side of the pavement, snacking on some olives, cleaning the surface of the bar, emptying tiny glass bottles of mixers onto spirit, throwing short jokes at the kitchen, swiping the broken glass on the floor, checking notifications on my phone, offering happy minutes to my fellow musicians.

A happy minute is similar to the concept of a happy hour but it just lasts a minute or slightly longer. The happy minute consists in refilling someone's glass for free during the minute of my choice. I created the happy minute concept to bring more smiles to people, so far it has been a great success.

Adam should arrive soon, along with Ellie and Cat, i keep on doing my job, explaining to French tourists that they have to come to the bar to order their drinks, taking swigs on my pints of water, tasting cheeses, smelling wines, washing my hands, swiping tables, re-organising board games in their boxes, pulling corks out of red wine bottles, pulling corks out of white wine bottles, unscrewing rosé bottles, rinsing towels, placing beer mats under glasses, placing glasses under nozzles, explaining the differences between a flat ale and a carbonated ale to customers, pouring more and more water, serving nuts, olives and cold food, typing on the till, typing on card machine, throwing coins into the till drawer, picking up change, thanking people, smiling, tapping out the rhythm of the music on the bar, laughing with Richard.

French has arrived. French is not actually French. People call him French because 'French' is his family name. French is English and because of his name, he is French. French is one of our chefs, he is a great cook, i think his family name brings good influence to his cuisine.

Outside the kitchen, French likes to rap and freestyle, he was born in London and grew up in a neighbourhood where great Grime artists have emerged. He's got the street credibility, the accent and the jargon that goes with it. French bumps my fist with his and salutes the guys on Jack's corner on his way to the kitchen. I hear him commenting, "Oscar! Long time no see! You're looking good bruv, you've lost so much weight! Your head looks bigger!".

In the kitchen, the guys and French are commenting on the extractor fan issue. I put down the little pile of plates that i just collected near the sink. The clock on the wall is telling me that Adam should be here shortly. I discreetly check the state of my shirt on the underarm area, bending my head and raising my elbow to estimate the damage my sweat could have done. Somehow, the wet patch is not as big as i was expecting. George witnesses the action and laughs, i laugh too and the other two are wondering what's going on.

"Guys, i've got a question" i
"What is it?" Yuki
"What's the thing with vinaigrette?" i
"What do you mean?" Yuki
"Why do we always serve salad with vinaigrette?" i
"Because it contrasts with the taste of the salad, it sharpens it, why? Did a customer complain?" Yuki
"No, no one complained, it is just me wondering, i think a salad is a salad, why does it need to be sharpened?

A bit of olive oil, a pinch of salt and pepper, perhaps a few condiments, vinegar is not necessarily necessary" i

"Don't you like vinegar?" French

"I prefer drinking wine, seriously, it is the same story with fish, why does it always have to be served with a slice of lemon?" i

"Same ting bruv, it sharpens it" French

"Well, i understand your knives have to be sharpened but salad could do without sometimes i believe" i

"Honestly, it would be a mad ting to serve a salad without vinaigrette bruv, people expect it, same with the fish and lemon, it's culture, customers would complain if we didn't serve it that way" French

"I get it" i

"We're talking about the majority, it's a bit like you not liking cucumbers, the majority of people like cucumbers, you have to adapt to the majority when you eat out" French

"Actually, how come you don't like cucumbers? It doesn't have a strong taste" Yuki

"Exactly! They are so bland! And worse, i can't digest them. If i eat some, my stomach protests, i burp, and then my mouth has to handle them! It is annoying" i

Adam enters the corridor, drops his bag on the rack and pops his head through the kitchen door. A communal cheer bounces against the walls, carried away by the big fans.

"Why is it so warm in here?" Adam

"The extractor fan broke" Yuki, George and i

"Damn, it's really hot!" Adam

"It is blistering hot" George

"Man that's crazy, have you been working like that all day?" Adam

"We have unfortunately, talking of which, could someone fill up the bucket with water and ice please?" Yuki

"Yeah, give me that bucket" i

"No, i'll do it, you go man, thanks for covering me today, i owe you a solid bro, thank you so much" Adam

"A solid or a salad? Without vinaigrette please, how did the shoot go?" i

"What? Yeah, it went well i think, thanks, but it was hot, we shot outside, it was a bit tricky with the sun" Adam

"Boys, seriously, stop complaining about the heat, all i've heard today is people moaning about the heat, it doesn't make any sense, you can't complain about the rain all year and then complain when the weather's warm, it's summertime, it's supposed to be hot, don't you think?" French

"Well, good thing you had the day off then eh? It's been a nightmare in here" George

"Guys, i'm off, i've got to be somewhere" i

"Thanks again bro" Adam

In the gents there is a hand dryer. I'm trying to dry the underarm of my shirt underneath it. It takes a bit of gymnastic bending to get into position below the shower of hot air, hopefully no customers will enter until i get both patches dry.

I get back to the corridor, i take my cardigan off the hook, say goodbye to the team, to the friends outside and to the customers i know with hugs, handshakes, waving hands and friendly nods. It always feels weird leaving the pub before closing time, it feels like going against the forces of gravity, breaking free from its magnetism. It takes a walk, almost until the end of the street to fully recover my sense of freedom.

Another magnet is attracting me, the date is calling. I am being absorbed by the near future against my will. I don't like it. It is as if every instant is being pulled forward, leaving no freedom of movement in the present. I should counterbalance that by allowing myself some resting time before arriving, this way i won't be acting like i am now, just travelling from one point to another with no joy in the transition. I could allow myself to be late, better late than sorry.

As of now, the main attraction of going on the date seems only to be the act of trying something new. I left the comfort zone, that's probably what it is, why i am not owning the moment. I could take long breaths, long breaths usually work well, let's just keep on walking.

Beside the bus stop, finally sat, i'm looking at the numbers on double deckers coming as if it was a lottery, waiting for mine to show up. I am on time, relaxed, my armpits are not showing signs of smelly rebellion but my legs are feeling a bit tired from the jog and the job. I am rolling a cigarette, peacefully sited on the ledge of a small wall, by the time i light it, the bus should be here.

Cigarettes can force you to take a moment to take a deep breath.

It is unpleasant that drop of energy i get sometimes after smoking. It always makes me feel stupid about myself for smoking. The bus arrives halfway through my cigarette. I drop and crush the rest of my rollie under my moccasin and go tap my card on the reader, i get a seat upstairs by a window. It's a new bus, made to look like the old ones with the stairs at the back. I'm wondering if tourists like to take pictures of the new red double deckers as much as they do with the older versions. Personally, i like the new ones better. Having spent hours sitting, reading, eating, sleeping, writing, listening to music in them makes these buses kind of a second home for me. But the change didn't make me feel nostalgic about the old ones. Apart from the fare that has doubled since i moved here, i don't mind the modernity. Bringing back the open platform at the rear of the bus is a great idea i think, it gives access to everyone, particularly to the ones who can't afford to pay for public transport. Personally, i would have added sleeping facilities. So many people take a nap on public transport, so many people pass out from exhaustion, it is not so eccentric to think that the designers would consider this aspect. Sleeping is underrated in this city. The thing with buses in London is that they remind me that surveillance cameras are omnipresent. Seeing my face or the top of my head on the screens during the journey tends to make me feel a bit self-conscious. Although, being potentially observed in an intimate moment like when i'm asleep is something i've got used to. I accepted being a character of the society's movie, i accepted the intruding technology. I even accepted that the things i say near my phone or the things i type on my laptop provide data that some companies sell without sharing the profit with me and without even clearly asking for my permission, i guess i'm quite a generous person.

There is a beer can rolling on the floor of the bus, it travels and bumps against seats and people's feet every time the driver brakes or accelerates. I would bet that if the new bus design had incorporated bins inside, it would have made no difference in the mind of the person who left that can on the floor. The next stop has been booked, someone has pressed the stop button, which is convenient for me because it is also the stop where i'm getting off.

Getting off that bus there takes a cat leap, aiming for the pavement with the best foot, landing as if nothing happened and keeping on walking. The transition and change of speed bring a funny feeling to the legs. There is no rush so i slow down my pace until i feel good about the tempo of my rhythm. Saturday evening street sounds are clashing against each other, silences have been completely silenced. The atmosphere is charged with excitement, early drunkenness and desire for something more.

I am not entirely sure what i am walking towards or what i am looking for, i just know that i am on time for the appointment. I salute the bouncer at the door, acknowledge his presence as he does with mine with a nod and a two line conversation then enter the bar. It is darker and less crowded than outside, i can't see any woman waiting on her own anywhere. No one is alone in here apart from me, i don't mind the solitary mode of being the first to arrive, apart from having to wait for the other.

I'd rather have patience than to have to wait.

My phone shows healthily charged batteries, i've got unlimited possibilities to keep me busy but i limit myself to a text message to inform Amy about my location and to ask her what she would fancy drinking. She says she is five minutes away, she is sorry, she is up for a Gin and Tonic. A Gin and Tonic makes sense right now, i'm ordering one for myself too. The barmaid comes towards me. Luckily, it is not busy and i don't have to battle trying to get her attention. It is kind of refreshing being on this side of the bar, it is pleasant having someone preparing the drinks for me although it takes away the satisfaction of doing it the way i like. Asking her to squeeze on the lime would be too adventurous i think. She's got the Tonic from a line, she doesn't have to pop bottle lids off, she presses on a button and easily fills up the two glasses but this system doesn't give her much room for style i must say. Holding the tube looks a bit lame to me. I'm glad we don't have those stupid pipes at the pub, they remind me too much of petrol stations. I can't tell if they are better for the environment, they certainly help not having to produce glass bottles but they could be made of materials that are harder to recycle, hard to tell. It is not always easy to be good with the planet sometimes. Two Gin and Tonics with wedges of lime, ice cubes and a straw, same combination as the ones i do at the pub but the price here is higher. I pay the total and leave a little extra to keep the culture of tipping alive. That's how it works, the barmaid gets tips, i get tipsy.

The door opens and a short cute woman walks in, she is walking towards me, she must be Amy. We're engaging with a hello, kissing each other on the two cheeks which makes me understand she is accustomed with the French way. She says she was expecting me to have bigger hair because of the way i look in my pictures on the app. I keep to myself that i was expecting her to be taller.

She is really thin and petite, quite sexy too. Her smile shows self confidence although her eyes seem to say something different. I'm wondering if it is sadness or a lack of sleep. She thanks me for the drink and we agree on a table at the back. She sits with her back against the wall, i sit on the chair opposite her with the open space behind me. It looks a bit like i am going for a job interview but i don't feel like having to sell myself. I like the way she sits and the way she holds her head. There is something attractive about her posture that is inspiring me to be relaxed.

"Is this your first time doing this?" Amy

"It is indeed, what about you?" i

"I do it a lot, it's kind of fun" Amy

"Oh yeah?" i

"I mean, it can also be unpleasant" Amy

"Have you had bad experiences?" i

"God yes, actually, one of them was with a French-man" Amy

"There you go" i

"I should tell you that i don't have high expectations for French guys, i dated two Frenchmen in my life and both experiences were pretty bad" Amy

"Merde, tell me more" i

"Well, the first one, we met briefly at a Gallery opening in Los Angeles one night and swapped emails, once i was back in London, he invited me for dinner" Amy

"Was he living in London too?" i

"That's the thing, no, he lives in L.A., and i wasn't going to go back there for a while so he invited me to a res-taurant in New York, to meet me in the middle" Amy

"Sure, i mean, it makes sense" i

"So he booked flights, a hotel and the restaurant for me to meet him in New York" Amy

"Did you go?" i

"Yeah, why wouldn't i? I like New York, the only weird thing was that he only booked one hotel room for the two of us, i didn't like that he was arrogant enough to expect a happy ending" Amy

"French people can be arrogant, probably the ones who live in L.A. too i suppose, and so you're saying it wasn't a good date? It sounds pretty extraordinary to me so far" i

"Not so much, the night wasn't great, he kept on inviting me over and over after that but i never went again" Amy

"Ah… and what about the other one? Was he arrogant too?" i

"The other French guy was horrible, some people don't even realise how misogynist they are, i'd better not talk about him, i actually left before the end of the date" Amy

"Did you?" i

"Yeah! See? You're at a disadvantage, it's gonna be hard for you to improve the image i have of French guys" Amy

"I see, it seems like a tough task, i am not sure i am fully trained for that" i

"So you mentioned in the messages that you like writing? What sort of stuff do you write?" Amy

"Oh yeah, i love writing, songs, books, anything that allows me to play with words" i

"Do you write books?" Amy

"I've only finished one so far" i

"What's it about?" Amy

"Well, it is about thirty days of my life in London, the idea was to reflect my reality during that period of time so i wrote it on my telephone, capturing everything that i was finding interesting around me everywhere i'd go during these thirty days" i

"Is it a diary?" Amy

"A little bit but it has different layers to it" i

"Why thirty days? What's so special about those thirty days? Amy

"Well, i had just got dumped by my girlfriend at the time and was trying to get out of the cul-de-sac i was into, these thirty days start at the end of November, they're leading up until xmas, as there's generally an excitement growing in the city during that period, i thought it would be interesting showing my perspective on it" i

"Did you write it in French?" Amy

"No, that's the thing, i wrote it in English, in my English, i thought that no English writer could write like me, they could never have that unconventional way of using the language. Now i'm not saying i am improving the image of the Frenchman with it but the least i can say is that my work is thoughtful and honest" i

"Did you find it difficult writing it in English then?" Amy

"One of the main difficulties is to accept to sound not very clever, it tickles your ego but it activates a humility muscle that is quite healthy in the end, but i've accepted that since i moved here" i

"Have you sold many copies?" Amy

"Well, i've self-published it, i've printed two hundred copies, gave a few and sold all the rest" i

"So you have another job on the side then?" Amy

"I work in a pub, i pour beers and share conversations, it's good inspiration for books" i

"It must be interesting" Amy

"What about you? What do you do?" i

"I create formats for radio, i used to be a presenter, i had my own talk show then i moved on to produce shows instead, which is what i am now, a producer, i earn a good living now" Amy

"Good for you, and how is it to create formats?" i

"Well, it's always stimulating to know your show is gonna be heard by a lot of people every week, it keeps me motivated" Amy

"Have you got to come up with different topics every week? Is it not too stressful?" i

"Yep, every week, the stress is ok, i get paid well so i guess the money makes me forget about the stress" Amy

"Fair enough" i

"But my dream is to make films..." Amy

"Oh yeah? To produce or direct or write?" i

"Sorry what?" Amy

"I mean, what would you do in the film, would you be the producer? The director? Or would you write the script?" i

"I see, sorry, i'm not used to the French accent, and yours is quite strong i must say" Amy

"I know, it's terrible" i

"No it's not, i hear it is very popular" Amy

"I know, i hate it though" i

"Why hate it if it's popular?" Amy

"I find it too thick, i feel it doesn't fit with the rhythm of the English language, it is not shaped for it" i

"I know what you mean" Amy

"So producer? Writer? Or director? Actor?" i

"Oh no, no, no, i would never be an actor, oh my god me an actor? No way, i want to direct, i'm taking a course at the moment to become a director" Amy

"I see, do you know what type of films you'd like to

make?" i

"Yes, it'll be between fiction and documentary, but i can't tell you any more about it" Amy

"Why not? Is it a secret recipe?" i

"It's a great story, actually, a true story someone confessed to me. Basically, i know it'll make a great film but i can't tell you more about it" Amy

"Wow, why? Is there a big revelation in it?" i

"No, not really, i mean, a little bit, kind of, it's someone's life and there are some really interesting angles to it, and no one's ever thought of making a film about it before" Amy

"It sounds exciting" i

"It is so exciting! I can't wait to start working on it again" Amy

"Have you worked on it a lot already?" i

"Not that much, i need to take some time off from work to really be able to focus on it, but i've talked to the person who the story is about and he's given me the go ahead to make the film, which is great" Amy

"That's cool" i

"Do you do any sports at all?" Amy

"I jog, i find it refreshing for the mind and good for the body" i

"I run too, but i hate it, i just run to burn fat, i find it quite boring, i should just eat celery instead" Amy

"Celery?" i

"Apparently celery has negative calories, it takes more calories to eat it than there are calories in it" Amy

"Wow, what if someone was getting addicted to celery?" i

"Nobody gets addicted to celery" Amy

"They should stuff burgers with celery, or create booze with celery, that would be great to be able to drink without getting fat" i

"It sure would" Amy

"Do you reckon it is why Bloody Mary comes with a celery branch? To balance out the calories of the drink?" i

"I don't know, you're the bartender" Amy

"Sure, have you got other tips as simple as celery to lose weight?" i

"I just watch what i eat, but i'm not too extreme about it, some of my friends literally read every ingredient on the packets of the food they buy, which i find ridiculous, because on the weekend they take some shitty drugs that are worse than any food on the planet!" Amy

"Ha yeah, good point! Oh man, sorry, just a moment, this is really annoying me, sorry" i

"What's wrong?" Amy

"I need to turn my phone off, some friends must be having conversation in my pocket and my phone keeps on vibrating, it is quite disturbing" i

"Do you mean you've got notifications popping up?" Amy

"That's it, that must be the effervescence of Saturday night i guess" i

"So you must have a lot of friends huh?" Amy

"I guess i know a few people, i mean, but what do you mean?" i

"Judging by all the notifications" Amy

"Oh i see, you know sometimes it just takes a small amount of French people to make a lot of noise, have you been to France?" i

"I've been to Paris but i'm sorry i didn't really like it" Amy

"Wait a second, are you saying you didn't like the city
or is it because of the people?" i

"The city, i find it too ostentatious" Amy

"Too what sorry?" i

"Too pretentious" Amy

"Ah, ostentatoire" i

"Os-ten-ta-toar" Amy

"Hey good pronunciation" i

"Haha really? No i'm terrible" Amy

"No seriously, you're doing ok with the 'r', try 'croissant'
for example" i

"Croissant" Amy

"That's cute" i

"I sound ridiculous" Amy

"No you don't, i mean, apart from when you say you
don't like Paris, who doesn't like Paris?" i

"Ha, well, i'm different i suppose" Amy

"Different is good, your glass is empty, would you like
another drink?" i

"Yes, that would be nice, but let me get them this time"
Amy

"It's ok, i'm closer to the bar" i

"No, i'll get them, a woman can get the drinks too you
know" Amy

"I know, well, maybe it is a reflex i have from working
behind a bar, but of course, ok, as you wish, thank you" i

"Same again?" Amy

"That would be lovely" i

She grabs her wallet and walks behind my back to the bar. I slurp my last drops of Gin and Tonic through the small black straw, leaving the wedge of lime in my glass like a stranded boat on the shore. Let's hope she doesn't have too much expectations about me. I can't tell if i feel attracted to her, maybe after the other drink my vision will be different. Did she imply that i was trying to impress her with my friends? I think she did, her tone was kind of sarcastic. Why would i try to impress someone with my friends? Do people do that? Is it a thing? Is it like driving a big car? Surely, that just can't be it, why would i brag about having friends? It is ridiculous.

"Here" Amy

"Thank you" i

"Have you ever seen the anti-drink driving advert with the bartender who does all the different voices?" Amy

"The what? Sorry?" i

"The anti-drink driving advert, it's an ad to convince people not to..." Amy

"Drink and drive, i see, well i'm not sure, i'm not well cultured with ads to be honest" i

"But it was a big ad, you must have seen it on TV" Amy

"Well, i don't own a TV" i

"You don't have a TV?" Amy

"No, i don't" i

"So what do you do if you don't watch TV?" Amy

"I don't know, i write, i make music, i go on a date with future film directors, there are plenty of things to do" i

"But there are so many amazing things to watch on TV, you have to catch up" Amy

"Honestly, i'm not sure if i'd enjoy it, i often get the feeling that TV is talking to me as if i was stupid, i've seen some TV games, they made me unsure about the whole thing" i

"But there are all sorts of interesting things on TV, what about Travel channels? Documentaries? What about sports?" Amy

"Ah yes, true, i'm probably fine with those" i

"Obviously, you're the artist type, i've got a couple of friends who are musicians, they hate television" Amy

"There you go, that must be it then, don't you find it too intense?" i

"Well, not really, i suppose it's kind of different for me cos i need to know what's happening for my work so i don't question it, and to be honest, it's always been part of my life, it's a presence, even if i'm not watching it, i like to have it on in the background, it keeps me company, it's like a friend" Amy

"A good friend? Or an annoying friend?" i

"Well, if it gets annoying i just change the channel, easy" Amy

"Do you like reading too?" i

"Yes i do, when i get a chance, which isn't often" Amy

"What was the last book you've read?" i

"It was a thriller called..." Amy

"Thrillers! Killers story, suspense, do you like to be scared?" i

"It can be quite exciting yeah, don't you think?" Amy

"Mmh, i'm more into stories about normal people rather than killers, no big drama but good conversations and not so many things happening, i'm not necessarily keen on stories about crimes" i

"But don't you enjoy being held in suspense? Having to find who the criminal is?" Amy

"To me it is a bit like eating a pistachio that has a closed shell, however long it takes me to get it doesn't make the pistachio taste better" i

"I'm sorry, what do you mean?" Amy

"I mean, why should i spend a whole film or book trying to find out who the bad guy is? I don't have much interest in studying how a bad guy does what he does, i'd rather watch the behavior of an interesting guy" i

"So what's an interesting guy for you? Or what is it that you do that you find interesting for example?" Amy

"Well, good question, i'm not sure" i

"Are you not?" Amy

"I am not entirely sure, no, but maybe i could tell you one thing, it is the learning process to become a better man" i

"How do you do that?" Amy

"It is about awareness, self-improvement, it is about curbing pollution" i

"Curbing pollution? Do you mean recycling?" Amy

"As well, but mostly with the thoughts" i

"Tell me more" Amy

"I do some exercises with my thoughts to help not pollute my mind, and when my mind is not polluted then i guess, i pollute less around me, if everyone was doing it, we would live in a more pleasant world i believe" i

"What type of exercises do you do? Now i'm curious" Amy

"Well, the idea is to catch yourself judging someone, because, as you probably know, when there's something you dislike about someone, it is often a thing you don't like about yourself right?" i

"Yeah i know but then what?" Amy

"When i catch myself judging someone, i try to judge my judgment instead of judging the person, it is more challenging and less degrading, instead of applying the judgement onto the person, i observe what it is that i don't like about the person or myself, and this way, i feel compassion instead of feeding negativity" i

"That's interesting, do you really do that?" Amy

"I try" i

"No, but come on, really?" Amy

"I try to but to be perfectly honest with you, when i'm in a shitty mood, it is almost impossible for me to do it, sometimes it's like i would even prefer to have some-one to moan about, but i always keep it in mind" i

"I like the intention, do you do the same when you see yourself acting like a misogynist?" Amy

"Misogynist? I can't imagine me acting like one but if it was to happen then i don't see why i wouldn't, it would be harder to notice though as i genuinely don't rate one gender above another, but of course it doesn't mean i never say things that sound misogynistic to the type of women who like to pick up on these things" i

"Well, that's a start" Amy

"Are you assuming that i am misogynist?" i

"I don't know you so i couldn't say, but considering the French guys i've met in the past..." Amy

"But you should also be aware of another type, we are a growing number of men that are in touch with our feminine side and that women should be able to trust to build a fairer society with, do you meet a lot of misogynistic people in your life?" i

"Are you kidding? Yes, everywhere" Amy

"Seriously?" i

"Seriously yes" Amy

"Really? Well it is hard for me to tell, to be honest, in my environment i mostly hear feminist opinions, not so much of misogynist chats" i

"That's because feminists have to raise their voices to be heard, society has been shaped by men and for men, we've got to react" Amy

"To educate men not to act like misogynists?" i

"That's one thing, yeah" Amy

"Ok, so maybe you could help me with this actually" i

"With what?" Amy

"Nuances that could make me sound like a misogynist" i

"Like what?" Amy

"I find it difficult sometimes to find the line, the line between acting like a gentleman and being perceived as a misogynist. For example, when i offer my help to carry something or when i offer my seat to a woman" i

"Well, it depends on the situation, the way, the tone, it is down to common sense but men don't necessarily have that" Amy

"Now that's sexist saying that" i

"No, it's a fact" Amy

"See, that's the thing i am not sure about with feminism" i

"What is it?" Amy

"It is in some ways tolerated if a woman says something sexist" i

"Men have been doing it for years and it has always been ok" Amy

"Sure, but it is a bit like saying that China should be allowed to pollute the planet because their industrial revolution came later and it would be unfair to ask them to reduce their emissions when we had our time doing it mindlessly" i

"I'm not sure if i totally understand what you mean, but the comparison seems a bit far fetched to me" Amy

"Ok, let me put it this way, why guys like me who see women as equal as men, or guys who don't mean women any disrespect because of their gender still have to get the blame? It is almost like we should feel guilty of being men or something" i

"At the end of the day you will still be men" Amy

"Could there not be a distinction, a name for guys like i just described? We could be recognised and accepted as a type of man that doesn't represent a threat, that understands the feminist viewpoint and would like to get on with things in a more relaxed way, it would be easier for us to build a fairer society without the touchyness of feminism sometimes i believe" i

"It takes longer than you think to tame a wolf into a dog" Amy

"A poodle, you guys want poodles and when you'll get poodles, i'd bet you'll complain about them not having a wolf tail anymore" i

"You're funny, it is not so simple, but if both sexes were to listen to each other equally, we'd be halfway there already, listening should be an easy thing to do, now men just seem to have more difficulty with it" Amy

"I'm listening to you right now" i

"You are yes, but, ok, let's put it this way, you're a writer right?" Amy

"Yes i am" i

"You must read books right?" Amy

"I do yeah" i

"How many books have you read that were written by women compared to the number of books you've read that were written by men? What's the ratio, roughly? Honestly" Amy

"Probably more male than female writers" i

"There you go" Amy

"But it doesn't matter to me, and i've loved books written by women, i don't buy a book because of the gender of the author" i

"By the way, reading all the Harry Potter books only count as one female author" Amy

"I haven't read Harry Potter. Look, i understand there is a fight women must lead to get more balance in society but like i said, i don't believe myself to be the type of man feminist women need to fight against" i

"There's always work to be done! Society has been run and organised by men, for the benefit of men over women, far way too long. Do you know how much suffering women have to go through? And i'm not even talking about periods or childbirth…" Amy

"Right, you may have more pain to deal with physically but you also get way more pleasure than us, i mean, sexually, you guys have a spectrum of feelings that is quite enviable" i

"Ha! That's a good point, ok, i'll give you that, but seriously, so much more has to be done in society, people don't know, that's why we need to keep on pushing, and we haven't even mentioned religions yet!" Amy

"I don't know much about religions" i

"I don't blame you, ignorance is bliss, personally, i prefer knowing, the more i know the better. I'm an information freak, i want to know everything" Amy

"A nympho-rmation freak?" i

"I'm interested in everything, i'm just very curious" Amy

"Like a cat" i

"Oh no, i hate cats" Amy

"Really? Why?" i

"They're horrible" Amy

"Oh come on, how can you hate cats?" i

"Cats are selfish, they're arrogant, they're fussy, they only do what they like, you can't trust them" Amy

"Surely you must find them cute when they purr, right?" i

"They are horrible nasty little creatures, they only come to you when they're hungry, they don't care about you or your feelings or anything" Amy

"Well, i really don't have the same opinion about cats, i think they're cool, is it not pleasant to watch them walk around?" i

"Oh no, i find the way they walk creepy, with their eyes, you don't know what they're up to, you just can't trust them" Amy

"Do you know many cats?" i

"Enough to know" Amy

"I've never met anyone who hates cats so much, that's interesting" i

"I much prefer dogs, a dog is loyal, it'll play with you forever. Dogs get my feelings and they listen to me" Amy

"Personally, it bothers me to see them with the leads around their necks" i

"Yeah, it is a bit sad, but they don't mind it, they're proud to walk beside you, they respect you, they like having a master" Amy

"What about when they are humping your leg? Is it not more than creepy?" i

"It is nature, it's normal if they feel horny, they've got to express it some ways" Amy

"What about when they eat dog turd? Does it not put you off?" i

"Oh that's disgusting, if there is one thing about dogs that i would change, that would be it, it makes me want to throw up just thinking about it" Amy

"Sorry i've mentioned it, but cats, really? Don't you even like kittens?" i

"Of course kittens are cute, but who doesn't like kittens?" Amy

"Ah finally" i

"So tell me about your love life, have you been single for a long time?" Amy

"Well, that's a question i ask myself sometimes and i am still trying to figure out how to measure it, if it has been too long or not long enough, to be honest i haven't been too proactive on that side, although it doesn't sound sexy saying that, i should probably tell you the opposite" i

"You don't need to, you're already French haha!" Amy

"It says enough doesn't it? What about you?" i

"Like i said, i like dating, i think it's fun" Amy

"Apart from when they're French right?" i

"Well, you're the best one so far i must say" Amy

"Thank you, that sounds almost like a compliment, maybe i should return it to you" i

"By all means" Amy

"You are so far, and by far, the best woman i have ever met through internet" i

"Because i'm the only one on your list! This is your first internet date! You're funny" Amy

"Sorry" i

"No, that was good" Amy

"That was true" i

"It is called a backhanded compliment" Amy

"A backhanded compliment? What's that?" i

"A backhanded compliment is a remark that sounds like a compliment but isn't a compliment, like you just did and i kind of did before" Amy

"I get you" i

"Right, i think i've got to go, i need to wake up early tomorrow" Amy

"Oh really? Waking up early on a Sunday?" i

"I'm gonna visit my grandma down South for a Sunday roast, there's a few hours drive" Amy

"Lovely" i

"What are you up to now? Are you going out tonight?" Amy

"I don't have anything planned, i think i am going to walk back home, i like walking, especially on a night like this one" i

"It was such a great day, so sunny, it's been amazing, you should defo enjoy your walk, that was your London summer, it's over tomorrow" Amy

"Hopefully it will last longer, it is incredible how it changes the city isn't it?" i

"I know, that is so true, why don't i live in a sunny place?" Amy

"Tell me about it, i come from the South of France" i

"Oh yeah, you're crazy, if i was from the South of France i would never come to live in England" Amy

"There is an average of three hundred sunny days per year in the city where i was born" i

"What?! That's mental, that must be the opposite ratio of what we have in London" Amy

"It is not that bad" i

"It is horrible" Amy

"Well, enjoy the Sunday roast if you can't have a Sunday rest, have fun with the Grandma" i

"Thank you, have a good walk home, it was nice meeting you" Amy

"Yeah, nice to meet you too" i

"Bye now" Amy

"Goodbye" i

There she goes, i take the road in the opposite direction. It's interesting how she dealt with the dating process and managed to finish the conversation so abruptly, i was just starting to warm up. I don't quite believe i'll ever see this person again. I don't see what is it we have in common. The similarities we seemed to have chatting on the app were greater than when being face to face, i suppose my mind was filling in the gaps. Perhaps this should be called a 'clatch", when you match online but clash in reality. I didn't have high hopes but i had imagined a better connection. At the same time, not knowing someone's voice and accent, someone's energy, someone's way of moving, someone's smell, it is not knowing much of a person. This online dating thing is too much of a gamble. It is quite clear, our tastes are too different, i don't feel we bonded either, i didn't even get inspired to make it sexy. Or perhaps the long seduction desert that i'm going through makes it harder for me to flirt, i must have lost some reflex. Anyway, i wouldn't bet on her liking my vibe, she doesn't like cats, she has a poor image of French people, she loves thrillers and TV, where would i fit in all that? Maybe i am selfish, arrogant with a creepy walk and i don't see it. I can't say that i was impressed by her either. Perhaps i am still not ready for a woman.

A sort of plastic box noise attracts my attention to my feet. I stepped on an abandoned ice cream pot, the type that comes from a burger chain. I assume that the person who left it on the pavement had the nice intention to keep the street cleaning employment going, like Liam. The customers of that chain are just too generous. I've got a bit of white cream on the brown leather of my moccasin and no tissue to wipe it off, no grass either, just concrete. The damage is minimal, i keep on walking. The road is extra large, it is massive and it goes straight a long way, this is Kingsland road. I'm going to walk all the way home, which offers a good amount of steps to experience sonder.

The smoke coming out of the grills, the couples eating at the tables by the windows, the clippers of barbers riding on heads, the neon signs of the shops, the queues, the outdoor smoking areas, the smell of alcohol, the stumbling walks, the crowded entrances, the security guys, the guest lists, the bags being searched, the stamps, the loud conversations, the loss of inhibition, the gain of confidence, the lust in the eyes, the shrunken skirts, the denim shorts, the tattoos crawling on arms and legs, the empty cans, the bus stops filled up with party people, the busy free cash points, the beggars working the night shift, the hands in the air calling for cabs, the people asking for directions, the people taking pictures, the vomit patches on the pavements, the noise of heels walking, the guys collecting cigarette butts from the floor, the police cars and ambulance beacon lights storming by, the taxis covered with ads, the hurried cars, the noise of glass breaking, the heads inside the internet shops, the people pissing in shadows, the drunk people sitting on the ground, the people shouting, the people shouting on their phones, the dealers cheers and offers, the plastic bags filled up with booze, the lit cigarettes in the night, the holes on trousers, the holes on T-shirts, the exaggerated laughters, the shine of lipsticked mouths, the pieces of meat in wraps, the crushed chips on the pavement, the trendy trainers, the stained white canvas plimsolls, the open shirts, the people dancing on the road, the people asking for lighters, the music coming out of the bars, the advertisements on telephone booths, the musicians carrying instruments, the people singing, the smell of weed, the mix of cultures, the people kissing, the people getting rowdy, the mini cab drivers, the Saturday night excitement, the music in the air, walking is good.

The road home, the sky changed outfit, sun almighty left to bring daylight on the other side of the planet. The lampposts are on but the light coming from the full moon makes them look almost useless. Garfield is welcoming me back, i high five him and slap the wall where his hands are drawn. A few steps further, i stop to have another look at the mural my neighbours painted this morning, appreciating the fact that i had an input in it and that it was designed for two French ladies. It is quite romantic, i am looking at all the elements in it again. Inside a room, a dog stares at a picture on the wall showing a desert landscape with a cactus, a rising sun and a hill which i don't remember seeing this morning. There's a leash on the floor, an open door and an empty dog bowl, with 'OH LIFE' written on it and further down 'what would i do without you' written in French. I guess the dog must be imagining the life he would have without his master, picturing it as a desert, because even though the door is open, and the dog isn't leashed, and he could leave, he wouldn't. If this piece is a demonstration of loyalty then the intention is very nice, such a big piece on a wall is quite a compliment, hopefully their French girl-friends will appreciate the romantic gesture and not be put off by being shown so much attention.

However, i don't see why there is no question mark at the end of the sentence...

'Qu'est ce que je ferai sans toi', 'What would i do without you' should come with a question mark at the end.

Unless it is used in the conditional tense...

Which would require an 's' at the end of 'ferai' and not without, like i wrongly suggested this morning...

"Oh putain! Merde!" i

This is my mistake, and now it is on the wall with the signatures of these guys at the bottom of the drawing. I remember that feeling of contentment when i told them this morning, i can't believe i didn't even think of the conditional tense. So now it says something different. It affirms: 'What i will do without you'. The dog is thinking of a trip to an exotic place on his own. He has managed to get rid of his leash and as the door is opened and there's nothing in his bowl to keep him interested, he is going to go discovering 'LIFE'. 'OH LA VIE', the dog is ready. The French girlfriends could be quite upset by such a decla-ration on a public wall. Oh dear, next time i see the guys, we'll have an interesting conversation i suppose.

Some music is coming from the other end of the road. The closer i get to home, the more bass i hear, the more distinct the melodies become. There seems to be a party happening at the ground floor of my building, some people are smoking by the door of my neighbours and others are standing in the middle of the road. They are congregating in a semicircle, i'm curious, i'm walking towards them, i'm nearly there, i should join in.

"Brémond! Fancy playing coin toss?" Neil
"Hi Neil how's it going?" i
"Throw the coin at the wall, closest coin to the wall wins all the coins on the floor, got it?" Neil
"Go on then, let me see if i've got some change" i
"I've got some 10p's or 20p's if you want?" Neil
"Wait a second, i actually got a 50p coin, alright, game on!" i
"Brilliant, come on join the queue amigo" Neil

"Yes!" one of the player cheers, she has just managed to get her coin very close to the wall. It is my neighbour Neil's turn, he takes a step back, rebalances his body, estimates the distance and tosses the copper. It bounces against the wall and rolls off to the pavement, "Shit!" he shouts. Another lady gets into position, she adopts another technique, lifting her arm as if she was playing pétanque, she aims and throws her coin quite awkwardly which makes everyone laugh as she doesn't even reach halfway to the wall. Next up is a tall guy, he looks Italian, he throws his coin with dexterity and gets the closest to the wall, even closer than the first girl's throw, she moans. Another guy is rushing to try his luck, Neil adds, "There's only one winner in this game, everyone else has to be a loser!". Someone appears from the open door, it is Dan, my ground floor neighbour. He comes to me as if we hadn't seen each other in ages, he gives me a hug and says with his Irish accent, "Hey! What's the craic man? Where have you been? Fancy a drink? Come here". I put my coin back inside my pocket and follow him inside, it would have been hard to beat the lanky guy anyway. The game is continuing like it started, without me.

The music is cheerful, a dozen people are chatting inside, perhaps some more are dancing in Dan's room closer to his speakers and DJ setup. Dan opens the fridge, grabs a beer pack and detaches one can from the plastic bracelet. His smile is on top form, eager to convey his joy.

"Pshit" Beer
"How are ya man, what have you been up to tonight?" Dan
"I went on a date with a girl i met on the internet. It didn't go too well. She didn't like cat people and i couldn't hide my tail" i
"Oh Jesus, online dating, i didn't know how much animals had to do with it" Dan

Someone puts a hand on my shoulder, i turn my head and see his housemate Charlie in a glorious state. He is sweating from his forehead and his shirt is wet, his eyes are intensely staring, peeled to the max. I grab his other hand and lean my shoulder towards his in a half-a-hug way. Another one of their housemates, Che, passes by with his boyfriend of the moment and says hi. Dan apologies and rushes to his bedroom, he heard that the song is about to end and has to lay down the following one. I notice a guy on the other side of the room near the old piano who i'd rather avoid as he often acts like he's got something to prove to me. I don't know if it is because he is a frontman in a band but somehow i seem to represent a form of competition to him. Almost every time we chat together, i have to witness a demonstration of his supposed superiority and wait until he feels better enough about himself to be able to exchange normally. It is tiring. I don't feel like going through the painful process of dealing with his ego tonight. That's an odd thing to do, having to reassure alpha guys, i accepted that, but it doesn't mean i can't avoid them.

I head towards Dan's bedroom to see how busy is the dancefloor. Someone comes out of it, it is a friend of his, i met him a few times before but can't remember his name. I salute him, he looks as excited as Charlie. I find the strength he puts in his handshake unnecessary but still i keep on smiling to him, he says he needs a drink, urgently. There are two girls and one guy dancing near the bed, i've seen their faces before but don't know them enough to interact with their improvised choreography. There's a couple chatting behind Dan, he's got his headphones on, mixing, i leave him to it and get back outside. Dan's girlfriend Holly enters the room with her mate, they are up for a dance, they are already jumping, we acknowledge each other with a smile and a quick hug as we're heading opposite directions. I follow my way out of the discothèque towards the front door. Zelda is sitting on one of the sofas, the one in an L shape that faces the mini bar made of wooden pallet by the entrance. I ask her if she enjoyed her sunny day off. She replies that she has emptied her sun cream tube, to make a point about how long she stayed outside on her chair. I congratulate her, "Excellent behaviour" i say, she wants to introduce me to a woman who is sitting next to her, "You should meet Susanna, she's gonna live here with her boyfriend for a few months, they're staying in Dan and Holly's room while they're away". I shake the hand of Susanna, her makeup is quite pronounced compared to what most girls would wear in the neighbourhood. It looks very well done, its elegance contrasts with the trainers and hoodie she is wearing. Susanna is Italian, she is from Tuscany she says, she is really pretty, she's got long dark hair and the average body size of a Tuscan woman. The nice tone in her voice attracts my attention, her laugh is friendly too. I instantly have a feeling like i've known her for a long time somehow, like we are branches of the same tree. It feels good talking with her, she is quite peaceful and she speaks French with an Italian accent that transforms some words into funny ones. Her boyfriend is French, which explains it all, he is the tall guy who was tossing coins quite well earlier. Looking at him again, he's got a nice light in his eyes too, i understand there is something special about these two as i feel a similar reaction in me with him when he comes shaking my hand. His name is Jules, he comes from Lille, where i used to live for some years. We raise the question about what spot in Lille we could have been in together at the time without knowing each other. I realise that it feels like i am more connected to these two than anyone else in the building.

"I love this neighbourhood, it is quite artistic, there are plenty of musicians around here, perhaps less than it used to be but still, the spirit is high. The bricks of these warehouses have soaked up so much melody over the years, there's a musical history in these walls" i

"Yeah, it's a real community, at least in this part of the road. This is Klaus, he lives in this house opposite us" Zelda

"Coin tossing isn't for me, hi guys, nice to meet you" Klaus

"Klaus is the daddy of the turf, tell them how good the people around here are" i

"Well, it is changing, yeah, the people change, but i don't dare give my real opinions about the people around here in Zelda's presence" Klaus

"Cheeky" Zelda

"Just kidding, it is a lovely neighbourhood with interesting characters and everyone brings something different, but still it has changed a lot" Klaus

"Was it better before?" Jules

"It is not comparable, for example, we used to have a gentleman coming to our door to bring free bread and pain au chocolats, these times are over" Klaus

"What? Really?" Susanna

"Yep, that's true" Zelda

"Yes, i can confirm, it was a golden era, although maybe not for this gentleman who had to wake up super early to go to work at the bakery. Let me have a go at coin toss" i

I leave my beer by the door and go queuing with my fifty pence coin in hand. A car slows down as it arrives near us, it is waiting for us all to leave the road to continue its way down. It is a taxi, a minicab, the driver doesn't seem to appreciate Neil's pleasantries. I didn't hear what Neil said but he usually comes up with funny stuff and telling by the laughter of the troup out there, i understand it wasn't bad. The car goes and we all get back behind the line. Everyone is trying to perfect his throw, someone manages to place a ten pence just a few centimeters away from the wall which sets the bar even higher. It is my turn so i try to focus on the weight of the coin, the distance and the height, memories of playing boules come back to my mind, coin toss suddenly looks like a pétanque substitute. I throw it with conviction but not enough accuracy and lose my fifty pence in the game. The suspense is still there, the space left is tight, it needs a strike of luck to win. Last one up is Neil's friend, the one with the pétanque strategy. Everyone is looking at the coin flying out of her hand towards the wall. It lands too far, game over.

There is money on the floor as if it rained cash. Charlie comes out of the door and attracts everyone's attention with his loud voice, waving a scratch card in his hand, "Guys, forget about coin toss, i'll show you where the money is!". He raises the scratch card in the air and adds, "I need some lucky fingers to scratch this card, i need someone who's going to bring me luck!". Charlie is staring at everyone frantically, his eyes look like they're going to pop out. He comes to me.

"The French flair, you're going to bring me luck!" Charlie
"I'm not sure i can do it, it is a big responsibility, what if i lose?" i
"You're not going to lose, i paid for the card already, it was only £2, it is all profits here" Charlie
"Mmh" i
"Alright, let's make a deal, i give you 10% of my winnings if you scratch it" Charlie
"10%?" i
"Yep, 10% of my winnings on the card if you scratch it now, here, use this 20p, it is a lucky coin" Charlie

I accept the deal, take the 20p, grab the scratch card and start scratching strategically so it tickles everyone's impatience. As it all goes, It reveals a gain of £2, which was the original price of the card. Charlie shrugs and continues laughing.

"Oh well, i haven't won but i haven't lost anything either, all good, let's play coin toss, give me my lucky 20p back" Charlie
"Hey, don't you remember our deal?" i
"Yes i do, i said i'll give you 10% of the winnings, but i haven't won anything, it's the same as the cost of the ticket innit?" Charlie

"Well, you said i would have 10% of the winnings on the card and that's exactly what it is, 20p is 10% of £2, you had a premonition and gave me what you owed me even before knowing the outcome, that's impressive!" i

"Bastard, it was my lucky coin" Charlie

"Ok wait, if you want, we can make the same deal again, i lend you this coin to have a go at coin toss and if you win, i'll give you 10% of the money you make at the game, same deal, right?" i

"Haha you French bastard, ok deal!" Charlie

"Here, play well man" i

"Alright everyone watch this" Charlie

Charlie starts the game and throws the first coin. He lands the 20p near the wall but not too near which stimulates everyone to have a go to try to beat him. The excitement is back on the playground, it is pleasant to find a communal entertainment outside for once. A few more people have joined the game since Charlie added the extra excitement but so far no one has managed to do better than him. Every time someone tosses a coin, the tension gets stronger around the game and every time Charlie makes more noise. The outcome is unexpected, Charlie's throw has won the whole lot. There is a total of £2.80 on the floor. He picks up the fortune and moans about having to giving it to me. I give him 30p and keep the remaining £2.50. I have just made £2 profit by investing 50p earlier. I could go on and lend more money now i've got some cash flow. It's funny how money makes money, maybe that's how the banking system was invented, with a wall on a street and a few throws.

I step back and bend to grab my beer from the floor by the entrance, fortunately, it is still standing. Zelda's long legs by the door are attracting my attention, the way she is sitting on the stairs allows me almost to see her underwear. I catch myself looking in their direction. It feels kind of wrong taking advantage of my angle of vision but her legs are delectable to look at and it is quite hard not following them to their conclusion. There is something captivating that is beyond predilection, it is like a magnet, it takes an effort to avoid looking at them. It makes me laugh internally, thinking of the possible ways Zelda could react to my irreverence if she saw me peering into her light summer dress. She would probably shout something degrading about men, giving a lecture on how women can't wear dresses on a warm day because men are just perverts, and how the continuous lack of respect inflicted on women is unbearable. I realise just now that the consequences of what i am doing could damage the atmosphere of the soirée. If she catches me i'll say, "If you show me your knees, i'll imagine your thighs but if you show me your thighs i won't imagine your knees".

Neil and Susanna are chatting by the door, they're both rolling the r's their own ways, Neil goes with the Scottish style, Susanna the Italian. Wally is sitting a few meters away from them by a hole near the building like he often does, waiting for a mouse to come out. I put my earnings in the smallest of my summer trousers pockets and invite my future neighbours to meet the cat.

"Hey guys, have you met Wally? Wally is the boss cat of the neighbourhood" i

"That's a big cat, what is he staring at?" Jules

"He's waiting for dinner" Zelda

"Hello Wally, what are you getting for dinner? Is it a pizza? Margarita? Quattro Stagioni? Fiorentina?" Susanna

"I don't think he is vegetarian" i

"Maybe he is flexitarian?" Susanna

"I've never seen him eating tofu" i

"Wally? What did you order? A burger? Fish and chips? Chicken wings? Is it a mouse hiding in this hole? Maybe he is just high, maybe he is on catnip" Susanna

"I'm wondering if it is the cat who is on catnip..." Jules

"Oh Wally, come here, come to Susanna, don't listen to this guy, he doesn't know how you get the munchies after catnip" Susanna

"He doesn't listen to you, he is too aloof" Jules

"Wait, maybe he is just feeling shy or awkward" Susanna

"Sometimes it is hard to tell if someone is shy or aloof but i don't think Wally is the shy type, you'll see when you'll live here that he gets everywhere like it is his own home, if you don't close the door of your bedroom he'll come to see what you're up to, he will spread pheromones and leave without showing much attention, you may dislike him at the beginning but then hopefully you will accept his personality, and eventually, you could end up loving him" i

"Yeah it took time for us to be friends but now we're good, he knows i love him" Zelda

"I feel closer to him than i was before, he often comes to

say hello by rubbing against my legs when i walk back home at night, sometimes i tell him about my day and he stays with me listening, i guess we're good mates" i
"Does Wally sell catnip to all of you?" Jules

Wally quits the spot and slinks under a car to disappear into Klaus's house as his front door is opened. Somehow, Zelda's joint ends up in my hand. I haven't smoked weed for quite a while in order to be more focussed on my projects. I haven't missed the high at all like i suspected i would before taking that decision to stop so i didn't really think getting back to it. It seems appropriate to let myself get a bit loose, i have been quite productive this week musically, i shouldn't feel guilty about not working on my songs tonight. I don't know if it is called a drag, a toke or a puff that i am taking from it but it is giving me a physical reaction. I've got the post doobie cringe, pulling a funny face like when i'm about to sneeze, with a sudden urge to go to the toilet. I totally forgot about these effects, i only seem to remember the good side of things.

"Shall we go in to listen to some tunes? Do you guys fancy a bit of a boogie in your future bedroom?" i
"We had a good one earlier but we must go home i think, got stuff to do tomorrow. We live in South London at the moment and it's going to take ages to go back" Jules
"Ok, well, it was really nice to meet you, ring my bell when you're around, we'll have a drink or something" i

They reply using the same words from different heights, he must be two heads taller than her and equally as chilled out as she is. The Franco-Italian couple sounds interesting, i look forward to seeing them again. I pass the joint back to Zelda and go straight to the bathroom, better be reactive when the smoke acts like a laxative.

There is a human thing that humans never want to talk about, even the ones who uses the word 'shit' a lot, even the ones who like to describe something great by saying 'that's the shit'. I guess i follow the same principle and won't comment here on what the Jazzy smoke has caused me to expel.

Sitting on the toilet emphasizes my relationship with my telephone. I am scrolling down pictures and videos of sunsets in London, friends drinking beers on Alexander's boat, friends on holiday by the beach, a new born baby, a drawing of a palm tree, combinations of skateboard tricks, attractive ladies, cats, friends behind turntables wearing homemade Daft Punk helmets at someone's wedding, a new arm tattoo, a stage-eye-view of a crowd, friends shooting a video clip, appetising homemade dishes, ballerinas en pointe, quirky buildings, quirky landscapes and a few selfies, i throw some likes here and there, being social from the throne of my ground floor neighbours.

There is a mirror above the sink, i realise my hair needs reshaping, it goes flat on the top and voluminous on the sides which gives me kind of a clown look, hopefully it was not as bad during the date. I wash my hands, stretch my arms and back and leave the bathroom, refreshed and relieved.

The music calls, i venture back inside to the bedroom. Dan is still behind the decks, between his two speakers facing the wall. One guy is sitting on the bed chatting with a couple beside him, there are two girls on the dance floor holding cans and vibing to the music. The tempo seems slower than earlier. My feet are tempted to move but it is mostly my head that follows the beat, my hips are a bit shy just yet. Dan turns his head, as he sees me, he asks if i could swap with him for a moment so he can take a break and roll a spliff. I ask him to show me his setup.

The disks spinning on the turntables are not real records, they are placebos, they are just there to recreate the vinyl touch for the DJ, it is the software that contains the grooves. There are thousands of songs in the computer which can all be played without having to flip a record and it just takes pressing one button to synchronise tracks together to the beat. So the DJing job has been simplified but still, it takes me out of my comfort zone. I put the headphones on and click on a song that seems to have already been highlighted in the playlist to try the system out. I play it in my ears first whilst the other track is still coming out of the speakers. Dan is laying a long skin on the shelf next to me and starts spreading tobacco onto it. I am shuffling the next track around, looking for the kick drums on the waveform, scratching the sound in the headphones, playing with the rhythm with my limited skills. Dan glances at the screen and gives me a sign to mean 'be careful with this one'. His facial expression tells me that he is trying to find a way to communicate with me so i take the headphones off my ears to listen to what he's got to say. I try to get closer to him but he shows me the palm of his hand to make me understand to wait. I am wondering what is wrong with what i am about to do. I am just playing with a kick drum, very basically but certainly on time, maybe he doesn't like me to scratch on his system. Dan picks up his phone and starts typing on it, he shows me the screen with the words he's written:

-'That track's by the guy who's sitting on my bed, just so u know...'-

As i see the message on his phone, i realise how it has got him into this state. I smile at Dan and show him a thumb while raising my eyebrows.
Things are easier when you can let yourself go innocently but now that i have this information, the whole process of just playing the next song sounds more complicated. I can't imagine the reaction this Dance music producer might have had if i played his track. He could take it as a stupid shout out, or a provocation, i don't know, the accident has been avoided but as we say in French, one train can hide another.

There are not many artists that i know from this list, it makes me feel like a tourist. I keep on scrolling up and down but can't find the spark, i see Gorillaz but their music may be too slow for the change, i don't want to scare off the two girls dancing behind me. Djing is more of an adventure than it looks when you have to assess music by the title of the songs.

What about Fatboy Slim? I could go with Fatboy Slim's 'Gangster Trippin'. I could start from the breakdown at the third quarter of the song and mix from there, although i will have to find something quickly to play after as there will only be a minute left to go and silence is not welcome here. I could just cue another Fatboy Slim track next like 'Weapon Of Choice', it could work. I'm not entirely sure but my gut feeling is telling me it will. I select the track, match the tempo with the current playing track and go to the part of the song i want. The excitement is growing, i'm focussing on the fader and the beat and do the shift as smoothly as i can.

'Come on, we got to kick that-kick that-kick that- kick that-kick that- kick that- kick that- kick that-
kick-kick-kick-kick-kick-kick-kick-kick-that-that-that-
that-that-that-that-that...'

I'm getting tickles all over from adrenaline as i let the music invade the speakers. Dan is smiling at me, he's finished rolling, he leaves the room, i don't dare look behind me yet as i need to prepare the next track, my hands are sweating, probably my back too. The music goes, more of my limbs are moving but i am still not fully liberated. I manage the cross over to 'Weapon Of Choice' but not as smoothly as i would have hoped. I am touching the equalizer knobs, opening and closing the gates, giving a little touch of freshness here and there. I have no clue for what to cue next. The 'what to play?' question is knocking at the door, it is accompanied by a friend called stress, i let them wait by the doorstep and choose to just enjoy the fun the current track is bringing at the moment for a moment, one must enjoy the present moment.

Someone is poking my shoulder, feeling my arm, it is that guy, Dan's mate, i still can't remember his name. He still looks very excited, his body language shows that he has an urgent request, that i must give him attention immediately so i take the headphones off and ask him to repeat what he's just said. He would like me to play a track that he is eager to dance to. The intensity and the neediness that the guy is showing make the whole thing suddenly unbearable for me, even the current song has turned insipid so i suggest him to play it himself and pass on the headphones to him. He accepts unapologetically and without saying thank you, he points his powdered nose to the laptop and starts looking for the title he wants. I leave the room quickly, before the guy seeks any types of assistance with the technology as i predict he will, judging by the way he is looking at the screen.

Charlie is dancing outside the bedroom wearing an ecstatic smile on his face. He is doing some moves that would be hard to replicate. His cheeks are red like most people tonight, difficult to tell if it is the result of today's sun or of intense dancing. He noticed i am looking at him so he comes to me.

"Do you remember that scene from 'Kickboxer' when Jean Claude Van Damme is dancing?" Charlie
"I don't watch action movies" i
"Why don't you watch action movies?" Charlie
"I don't understand them" i
"But there's nothing to understand in action movies" Charlie
"That's exactly what i mean" i

A new face pops in, a blond woman i didn't notice when i entered, she joins the chat, her shirt is slightly open, she's looking rather pretty.

"Sorry to interrupt, have you guys got a lighter please? I think i've lost mine" blond woman
"I have one, here" Charlie
"Hey! That's my lighter!" blond woman
"Is it really?" Charlie
"Yes it's mine, i was wondering where it was" blond woman
"One never really owns a lighter" Charlie
"This one is mine" blond woman
"Why would it be yours?" Charlie
"Because i had it when i came here" blond woman
"But you didn't buy it, did you?" Charlie

179

"Well, no i didn't but i brought it from my house" blond woman

"That's what i mean, you never really own a lighter, nobody does, it always ends up in someone else's pocket, think about it, have you ever managed to keep any basic lighter you bought brand new until it runs out of gas?" Charlie

"I don't think so" blond woman

"That's what i'm talking about! Lighters belong to nobody, they just go from hand to hand, pocket to pocket, so this is not your lighter, this is a lighter and you can have it if you want it but still, it won't be your lighter" Charlie

"Ok, can i have it then?" blond woman

"There you go, but hey, remember, lighters are free, they never belong to anyone" Charlie

"I think i've got it now, thanks" blond woman

"No worries" Charlie

"Do you live here?" blond woman

"I live upstairs" i

"That's quite convenient" blond woman

"Yeah, i didn't need to go too far tonight for a boogie" i

"Lucky you, i live in West London, i'm a friend of Che who lives here, we work together" blond woman

"Ah ok, cool" i

"Don't you love the crystal palm trees? Che brought them didn't he?" blond woman

"Yeah he did apparently, they're unbelievable, that's crazy how big they are" i

"I know, he got them from a shoot we did at work, i'm so jealous" blond woman

"They look great, two meters high crystal palm trees,

two of them as well, i remember when i saw them for the first time, i couldn't take my eyes off them" i

"Are you French?" blond woman

"I think so" i

"Oh..." blond woman

"Is it a bad thing?" i

"Oh no, i am not xenophobic, i'm too bad at geography to be xenophobic, my housemate is dating a Frenchman, she says he is a great lover" blond woman

"That's nice to hear, and you, where are you from?" i

"I'm from Sweden" blond woman

"Hence the blond hair" i

"Yeah, we're all blond, it's kind of boring, are you from Paris?" blond woman

"No i'm not, i'm from the South" i

"Oh i love the South of France, i love St Tropez, are you from there?" blond woman

"Not too far" i

"Oh that's lovely, my friend owns a flat there, we go during summertime sometimes, it's great" blond woman

The music stops. It restarts again, i am guessing that's the track the guy wanted to play.

"Oh i love that song, wanna go for a dance?" blond woman

"I'm alright for now i think" i

"Come on, let's dance, this track is so good" blond woman

"You should go for it, i've just had a session, i'm good

for now" i
 "See you back here, my name is Stella" Stella
 "My name is mond, Brémond" i

Melodies tend to repeat themselves, i walk towards the end of the living room to have a closer look at the palm trees, caressing the beige keys of the old piano on the way. Palm tree leaves made of crystal, they would look even more dramatic if more lights were aiming at them. They're fabulous, they combine the sparkly reflection of the sun on the sea and the coolness of the shape of palm trees. I'm going to sit on the sofa beside them and imagine that i'm on a beach.

Closing my eyes, letting everything go, it has been a long day, i'm savouring a well-deserved moment of solitude. It was a bit funny going on that date earlier, i'm glad i did it. I'm glad i had not built big expectations before going. It really didn't click, you can't force a click, there is no point wasting her time or mine i suppose. She is quite sexy though but if the sex flows like the conversation we had, i'm not sure it is worth trying it.

Falling into sleep, one of the luxuries of life that i treat myself with every day. There is nothing truer than falling asleep, to shrivel up until it all goes. I love the feeling and i would probably enjoy it even more if i had achieved something bigger today. Nonetheless, it still feels good to fall asleep on the neighbour's couch during a house party by a crystal palm tree on a warm summer evening.

"Oh someone is sleeping" Zelda says as she is walking by.

"I am not sleeping, i am thinking i think" i

"Very deep thinking i imagine" Zelda

"I was contemplating the palm trees and they led my thoughts elsewhere" i

"They look amazing don't they?" Zelda

"Absolutely" i

"I love these palm trees" Zelda

"You're pretty lucky to have such palm trees in your living room, i've got one upstairs but it is not made of crystal" i

"What is it made of?" Zelda

"It is made of palm tree" i

"You've got a real one?" Zelda

"Yeah but i'm not sure if it's still alive" i

"That's a shame" Zelda

"I found it in the neighbourhood, it was laying flat on the ground, down the road at the back, on the pedestrian passage, it was just there so i took it" i

"But how bad is it?" Zelda

"Well, it still has leaves, i've planted it in a pot but some leaves are drying out and falling off so it is hard to tell if it will live for much longer" i

"It doesn't sound like it is on top form yeah" Zelda

"I mean, i'm not an expert at planting plants, i don't even know if it was dead already when i picked it up, you know, it was on the floor, i don't know how long it had been there for, i don't even know how long palm trees can survive with the roots off the ground, i suppose longer than a fish outside water but still, it is hard to tell" i

"See this plant on the ledge? it was dying when i found it and look how strong it is now" Zelda

"But how bad was it when you got it?" i

"It was pretty dry, there was just a stem and it was way thinner" Zelda

"You must have a resurrecting power, that's amazing, that's wonderful, is that what it is to have green fingers then?" i

"Perhaps, but you just need to give it some good soil, some water and some love, that's all" Zelda

"Brilliant, do you reckon you would be able to save my palm tree too?" i

"I don't know, i can try" Zelda

"If you could have a look at it someday and give me some piece of advice or make your magic work on it that'd be great" i

"Sure, i can have a look" Zelda

"I'd love it if it could rebirth, palm trees remind me of where i come from, i find them inspirational" i

"Hey let's have a look at it now if you want, you've got it

upstairs right?" Zelda

 "I do yeah, now?" i

 "Yes why not" Zelda

 "I don't want to disturb you from partying" i

 "That's fine, i've had a fair bit of dancing already, i'm
 happy to" Zelda

 "Really?" i

 "Yep sure, let's do it" Zelda

 "Oh nice one, cool, yes" i

I stand up by the crystal palm tree, raise my arms up to stretch my back and stretch my jaw and neck with a yawn, "You're such a cat" Zelda says. Somehow the atmosphere has changed since earlier. Dan is back DJing, people are still dancing in the bedroom, but the volume of the music sounds lower, even outside is empty, a neighbour must have complained about the noise. I'm wondering how long i had my eyes closed for.

I'm waking up for the second time today, everything is slow again. I slide and spin my key inside the lock of the building door, it opens. I'm leading the way up the stairs because i'm the man, it would be rude following her, my head would be at her derrière level and i don't want to challenge her feminist views so much. I'm appreciating the post-nap slowness of my mind and i don't feel like getting into her type of battle of principles right now. She likes those too much. She jumps on every chance just to affirm her position. I don't know her star sign but i can tell it is one that contains fire.

"I've never been upstairs" Zelda

"Have you not?" i

"No, never" Zelda

"Really? Have you never been to a party?" i

"I would remember i think, but i haven't been living downstairs for that long" Zelda

"We rarely do parties anyway, it is rather quiet upstairs" i

I slide and spin my key inside the lock of the second floor door and we enter, the kitchen lights are on, Chloe and a friend of hers are sitting by the big table having a drink.

"You guys have a table tennis table, that's great!" Zelda

"Do you like playing ping pong?" i

"I'm not really good but i like to play, although i'm very competitive and i hate losing" Zelda

"Oh really? I'm wondering why that doesn't surprise me, hi guys, have you met Zelda?" i

"Of course, you live on the ground floor don't you?" Chloe

"Yes we've met, you came down one day to collect a package didn't you?" Zelda

We take the steep staircase up to the roof terrace, i go first again, Zelda follows without commenting about the steepness like people usually do when they climb it for the first time, so i keep walking until the door as normal. We get on the roof, the full moon is doing a great job of lighting the décor.

"That's the London eye over there, it is looking at us from the corner of the eye" i

"This is a great view" Zelda

"You should see how the view looks like from the top floor of that building, it is amazing" i

"This one just here? I love that building, with the outdoor fire escape, it is so Brooklyn isn't it?" Zelda

"I can't believe how bright it is tonight!" i

"Well, it is full moon and there isn't even one cloud, if you just look at the sky, you wouldn't believe you're in London" Zelda

"True" i

"We should be able to see shooting stars on a summer night like this one" Zelda

"Yeah?" i

"Yes, come on, you can't have such a beautiful sky and no shooting stars" Zelda

"Of course" i

"Where's the tree?" Zelda

"Over there look" i

"Aw, it is so cute" Zelda

"You see these dried out leaves on the floor and these ones getting yellow? That's not good is it?" i

"I see, but hey, it is in better condition than i was imagining" Zelda

"That's good" i

"The pot might be too small though, there is not a lot of soil in there" Zelda

"Do you think so? I've potted it in this one because i

thought it would look good but i didn't think of soil proportions too much i must admit" i

"Fashion first! Let me pull off the dead leaves, it's going to help" Zelda

"Sure" i

"So, i would replant it into a bigger pot, i would add some good soil to it, water it and see what happens" Zelda

"Ok, that's great, thank you very much" i

"You're very welcome, i don't see why it wouldn't live" Zelda

We stand up and walk back slowly towards the door. I feel something. There is something in the air that is calling my attention. A form of electricity, a wake up call. I'm wondering if it is coming from her, from my imagination or from the moon. I look at her again, neither her mood or her body language seem to have changed although i'm sensing some types of arousing waves. She could be sending them i don't know, but if she does, then i'm curious to know what she means. The scene and the scenery are too beautifully lit not to inspire romance, she looks attractive under this moonlight, more attractive than under the sunlight for some reason. Something clicks, after six months of silence, by the magnetic change in the energy field, my sexual being is brought up to my awareness, unleashing itself from my usual uninterested and solitary mode. It is asking me to react, to be aligned with it, to consider that it is not only the palm tree that requires attention. I understand from this inner call, that a part of me has been shut down and ignored, that it wasn't necessarily mindful of me to repress my sensuality for so long.

I should open myself and embrace this electric feel, see where it wants to lead me to. It seems to make sense to follow this instinct tonight, i can't see no shadows of regretful consequences obscuring the way.

She is already near the door, ready to go back downstairs. I should check with her, i should do something.

It is hard to see beyond the wall of her strong feminism, she almost makes me feel guilty for my intentions. If we knew each other better then perhaps i could think of something more suitable but right now, considering what i know of her, i fear the only thing i would get in response, is a sermon on the cliché of the typical Frenchman who only has sex on his mind and on the fact that a woman can't go to a private space with a man without being sexually solicited. I haven't seen any real signs from her, it might all just be a trick from my mind. Although i've got this feeling. This electricity in the air, i experienced it before. I know that feeling but it is hard to tell if it is only coming from me. I need more time to assess better. I slow my steps down. I need her to come back, to be in the not-so-close-to-the-exit zone, i need to do something before she pushes the door. She is pushing the door.

"But hey, what size pot exactly? That i should get, do

you reckon?" i

She stops.

  "Does it have to be proportional to the size of the roots?
  How big are they going to grow?" i

I walk back towards the tree pretending to study the case
again, she steps back and walks back to the tree too, i
have gained a moment.

  "I don't think you need a huge pot, just get one that has
  enough room for the soil, unlike this funky little one"
  Zelda
  "Like how big?" i

She comes back to the palm tree with me, i get into squat
position, securing more time to read between her lines.

  "I'd say that big, you don't need more than that" Zelda
  "Ok and is it better if it is in terracotta or ceramic?" i
  "It doesn't really matter, the soil has to be good though"
  Zelda

It is hard to find more technical questions to make the
conversation last. I am trying to study the situation the
best i can, i let her woman waves invade my way of
understanding the world to grow up as a man, i listen to
my feminine side too. I can't sense any awkwardness nor
tensions from her side. I can't tell about her feelings, she

seems perfectly placid, her British coolness is unscanna-
ble. If i simply show her my intention, her reaction will
allow me to know. Her response could be quite tough but
i'm sure i can take it, i'm a man after all. Perhaps not the
type of man that feminist women complain about, but i'm
still a man.

"Ok, and do you think, it needs chopping a bit?" i
"No, no, just take off the dead leaves like i did when you
see any, that's all" Zelda

This conversation has clearly reached its end. We stand
up, she is looking at the sky again, i still can't tell whether
the arousal is only on my side. It is quite present though.
I must go for the kiss and see. I must say something to
introduce it. I need a good line, something more witty
than sleazy, something to get us out of our neighbour-
ly politeness, something to cross the boundary. I need it
now. I'm rushing through my mind to find something that
could do the job but the situation has turned it all blank.
I feel short of words and yet not so awake. It is now, she
hasn't walked back yet, i need something to say, i can't
just kiss her straight away with no introduction and no
signs from her. My mind is going everywhere it can but
i can't find the bridge from the pot conversation to the
kiss. I just can't thank her for the advice and kiss her. It
would be so bad, although it could do the job. It doesn't
matter what i will say, either we kiss, or we don't.

No, i can't see myself going from 'thank you' to 'kiss you', this is not happening. It makes me cringe just thinking about it. What else could it be? I need something to bounce on. My mind is going slow but my thoughts are boiling, if only a bubble could pop with an idea. I need something appropriate, something nice and not ridiculous, something i could potentially be proud of, something smooth, something honest that doesn't mess too much with my notion of respect, i need something that works, whatever it is, i need something now.

...

That must be how miracles happen. When you intensely wish for something, the universe brings it to you. All of a sudden, coming from the sky, from light years of travelling the dimension of space, entering earth's atmosphere at great speed, just on time for its cue, a meteor shows up. Zelda shouts, "Yes! I've just seen a shooting star!". It breaks the silence and unknots my tangled thoughts, i finally see the light. I follow my inspiration, conforming to my instinct, purposefully ignoring my own judgement about the quality of what i am going to say, knowing it is just the matter of doing it and that action speaks louder than words. "Ah voilà!" i say and lean my head towards her to kiss her.

She lets me kiss her and we touch tongues like people shake hands for agreement. The kiss lasts long enough for me to understand that she is not going to reject me. I touch her back, making the natural ascending move to her hair and place my other hand on her hip. She passes her fingers through my hair, sliding up her hand until the nape of my neck, digging her fingertips in with short nails. I am not sure if i am focussing on her hair, her hand in my hair or on our mouths playing together. I let the flow guide me, i am not starving, i'm just enjoying every moment of this kiss that is unexpectedly lasting. Her hand leaves my neck and goes down to my bum. She lands on it like a bird on a window sill. She is examining it, squeezing in a circular motion so it doesn't feel like squeezing. The two mouths intensify the pressure, the hands follow the intention, her breathing gets sensual, her warmth is surprising. I put a palm above her bra and summer dress, pressing harder as she does too. She slides one hand over again, this time, to politely feel my crotch on her way down to my leg. She may have felt a reaction down there, a signal of resurrection. Her breast seems less shy, we're re-focussing on an intense kiss until slipping off each other's lips. We de-smack, the moon is making her mouth shine generously, her eyes have changed impression, she is smiling. She comes back to me and kisses me again, shortly and with a new intention, i don't get what her intention is. She pushes me back like she is rejecting me, as if i had done something wrong.

We are a meter away or so from each other, i am dealing with the suspense peacefully, wondering if she stopped because she realised it was a mistake or if it is the last kiss that made her retract. If it means an end to our moonlit tryst, i am cool with it. I'm enjoying the satisfaction of having been out of my comfort zone, pleasantly surprised by the way she reacted to my inspiration. I'm wondering what she is going to say.

She says, "Wait".

Her 'wait' can lead to anything at this point but it doesn't bring much to the conversation. I don't necessarily feel like talking anyway, my mouth still feels impregnated by hers, i'd rather make the sensation last. I'm still waking up and i am actually quite relieved not having to think of something to say anymore.

She takes another step back, now we have fully recovered our respective personal space. I am watching her, patiently, silent, the visual is loud enough. She raises her arms in the air and aims for her back. She is working behind her shoulders. She catches the zip of her 60's dress and zips it down in two goes. She slides her hands down to the bottom, grabs the end of the dress and pulls it all up above her head tactfully so her hair doesn't get upset with it. She raises her chin and throws the vintage dress to the floor.

I am standing still on the roof, stunned by her move, looking at her body in her lace turquoise underwear, holding my jaw. She is standing in her boots as slender as a

Fender. Time has stopped like it never existed.

"It feels better like that" she says, i nod and smile to agree. She steps forward towards me, 'It feels better like that' echoes in my head. I'm opening all my pores to receive her fully, photographing the eroticism of the scene in my mind so i can remember it later. She looks too sexy for the neighbours' windows around, if anyone is watching, they can probably see her derrière lit by the moonlight. There's a woman in her turquoise bra and thong touching my chest, she is dressed like i should roll my arms around her to warm her up but the weather has done the job already and we are not really close sentimentally. I delicately adjust my moves to a slightly slower tempo, slower than the previous kisses, letting electricity build the foundation of our inevitable but still unpredictable intercourse. I grab her derrière firmly so she knows that i consent.

Here, on the roof, where the magpie picks leaves and the cat slinks across, where guitars sing melodies and ideas float around, where grapefruits shine under the sun, where the rain beats down during the month of July, here, by a young rescued palm tree, i am standing with a woman in her turquoise underwear, bathing in moonlight.

Instinctively, i stick my canines into the skin between her shoulders and her neck, to reassure myself she's real and to cool down my excitement. My hands on her nakedness, following her lines, letting nature guide my moves, i grab her jaw and cheeks to kiss her with more control as a response to her temerity. I'm gonna bite her lips but she escapes to kiss my neck. A sensation of cold and wet appear on my skin where her mouth is teasing me. I raise my head and look around, imagining how i should make the situation evolve harmoniously. The red bean bag is on the side like an accomplice, i pull back, take my cardigan off and throw it onto the giant outdoor cushion, it roughly lands on it. I am trying to add some discretion, i don't need to attract anyone's eye or camera to the scene but she doesn't seem bothered by the risk of being seen. The moonlight is so strong tonight, her moon must be flashing the building behind. It's not exhibitionism until someone watches, hopefully everyone is asleep and stays asleep.

She understands my move and goes to lie down on her back on my cardigan. I follow her, she is looking at the beauty of the sky again, commenting on the number of visible stars as she is opening her legs. I go down on my knees between hers. She pushes on her arms to sit up straight and grabs the top of my trousers to undo my belt. I pull up the bottom of my shirt to make it easier for her. Zelda pulls on the belt without skipping a beat, i raise my chin, it is my turn to look at the exotic sky. I am staring at the stars while my fly is being undone. The touch of her hands is reviving me, she stretches out the elastic of my underwear to pass it over my growing physical reaction. I'm getting harder naturally, in the air, on the roof, on my knees, in the most unexpected situation. She grabs my part to direct it to where tough lectures occasionally are aired, and with her other hand feels the underneath. She tightens her lips, her tongue is moving too. She accelerates, acting greedily, generously but in a selfish way. I want to stroke her hair but it seems useless, she is shaking her head too hurriedly so i keep my hands playful all around, feeling her neck, back and skin, catching her jaw to make her slow down, caressing her lips with my thumb as they are surrounding the most telescopic of my organs. She slows down and accelerates again, i guess she wants intensity, she plays all around like people do with an ice cream when it is melting. My fingers are going between her thighs, trying to reach the junction of her legs. The front side of her thong feels coldly wet, i want to get behind it but the position we're in doesn't really let me. Still, i want to play too, giving pleasure is pleasurable. I pull back and push on her head so she lies flat on her back, she moans, the nuance in the tone sounds too naughty for the possible curiosity of the neighbours. I know enough people around here to become self-conscious, it distracts me from totally focussing on her, i quickly look around to see if anyone's head is popping out of a window. All quiet so far, so i pursue the line of her thighs with a hand on each leg, they come together to attract me to an abyss of desire. I get to her centre, i move the triangle of fabric and let the ambient air make the first contact. She wants intensity in the friction, not a slow build up, so i adapt to the speed. She invites the longest of my five to disappear inside her, i keep my thumb on her button. She makes sounds that ignite me further. She is grabbing the sides of the bean bag, letting her head fall out on the other end like she didn't need it anymore, like nothing mattered apart from what's happening around the middle of her body. Into motion, my hand is going East and West and North, feeling her reactions and her inside, i insert another one. She moans a bit louder, the open windows of the buildings around absorb the echoes. I slide my left hand over her belly up and pull off her bra half way down her right breast, trying a melody, the other side is calling but i keep my right hand playing the chords.

She reaches for my hand on her nipple, she clenches it and uses the other to push on the floor to raise her head towards me. She orders, "Please get a condom, now". I am observing the urge without questioning it. I guess when a woman shows that much hunger, there is no point serving her too much of an entrée.

"I'm back in a minute, please do not move, you are perfectly lit like that, if you could see what i see from here, you'd love it" i say, catemplating the lines of her feminine body. She laughs and lets her head fall back again, her chest is wide open, revealing ribs to the stars with a part of her bra roughly placed. I had never looked at this red bean bag as a jewel cushion before. I recover my hands, bend down and bite the innocence of her right flank, just to say bye for now. It feels tender under my teeth. I clench my jaw slowly even though she seems in a hurry. Somehow, i find in biting a way to release pressure from desire, to cool down my mind, to conduct the electricity adroitly.

Teeth unclenched, i slide my lips to kiss her belly under her belly button and kiss her further down just above the border of her turquoise sea. I bend a bit more, go closer to the shore. She slides her fingers through my hair and catches some curls to stop me, "Ok i'm back in a minute, my room is just there, please don't move" i say and pull my head back.

My knees feel a bit sore as i stand up, i didn't realise in the fever of the action that the ground is quite rough. I pull my trousers up and cover my excitement with my shirt, walking like i had stolen something. I prudently venture to my bedroom, open my door, making the wall shake. I walk to my bed and reach behind my lamp where the collection of condoms have been sleeping for months. I take another cardigan, a thicker one, this one will be for my knees, if i am going to have sex outside, i may as well enjoy it more comfortably. I walk back out, a bit rushed by the eagerness to keep the momentum going but i'm not in a hurry, still walking funny with my unbuttoned fly. I lay the cardigan on the floor and open the square shaped condom package.

Zelda is still there with her head in the sky. I go back to the position i was into, i am still hard but could be harder. I test the condom to find out which way it is going to unroll. I pinch, and little by little push on the single finger glove down the baton of love. Putting a condom on is like raising your own flag, there is a solemn sensation when it is all erected.

Zelda arches her back to remove her coloured underwear. She takes it down to her boots and with a little leg and hip coordination, gets them out of the way. She reopens to me like a capital M. I put my right hand on her belly and with my thumb reach for her flower. I hold myself, pointing towards her, the condom cuts down sensitivity, it is not unreasonable to assume that men get less sensations than women out of this safety deal. The moment is near, it is on her lips. I can barely feel her inner warmth as i push into her, but the way she reacts inspires me to keep on going forward. She is moaning sounds that compliment the situation, her breath is louder, i have almost forgotten about the neighbours.

Silently, i come out to re-organise the tight ring of latex so my blood can flow better and introduce myself again. The more i enter, the more she feels, the more she moans, the more it grows, the more i feel, the more she feels, the more she moans, we're getting in the loop.

Back and forth, slowly, feeling her inner sides softly.
Feeling her inner thighs on my hips, reading her feelings on her lips.

Recovering, rediscovering, with a kind of instinct that was extinct.
Incentive, sensitive, in touch.

Sensual collage, massage, soothing flesh.
Sliding on her strings, bending notes, unknotting knots.

She opens her lungs, she wants it fast while i want it to last.
I'm catching up with my libido.

Wet, sweat, chest.
Healing heat, therapeutic, healing beat.

Precipitated, precipice, simmering iris.
Contorting bodies, improving melodies, changing chords, stretching vowels.

Forth and back, giving, giving like a man i am, clenching, back.
Public display of imperfection, power chords, forth.

Itch, twitch, tilting, switching, knees, repositioning, in transit.
Interrupted dance, disrupted cadence.

Her back against my chest, my paws on her breast.
Nipple, stapler, breath in, out.

She uses the 'f' word, i use a French word.
Immersed, containing my thirst, quenching hers feels better than coming first.

Pumped veins, vascular, muscular, pressure.

Volatile passion, agitation, liberating labour.

Giving, giving like the man i am, moving my hips like an animal.
Adrenaline, alive, revival.
Storm, exclamation, collision.
O renaissance, i need to stay immobile for a moment.

Breathing, slowly coming back from mental numbness, my vocabulary seems to have vanished, from any languages. It is almost impossible to express myself, but everything seems to make more sense, satisfaction speaks louder than words. I am relieved of a weight i didn't suspect to be that heavy, telling by how light i currently feel. Yes.

"Yes" i
"Hum?" Zelda
"Yes is the word i was looking for" i

We laugh and get back to a more respectable position, more like neighbours. Zelda says she should go back downstairs to the party, she is naked in her boots, sitting on the outdoor giant cushion. I slip out of the condom, relaxed, swollen and shining. I do a knot to the rubber glove and put it inside my pocket like a tissue. "My penis is a warm gun" i sing, borrowing The Beatles' 'Happiness Is A Warm Gun' melody. She is giggling, pulling on her turquoise strings. I stand up, re-organise my clothes around my hips, my knees are feeling a bit numb. She is putting on her bra, clipping it behind her back without trouble. I bend to pick up her summer dress from the floor. Zelda grabs my hand and gets up. I prepare the dress above her head and let it fall on her shoulders, she waves her arms into it and lets it go down on her body with a wiggle of her hips. I want to pull her zip back up but she is faster than me.

"Thank you, i think i can sort that out myself" Zelda
"Of course it is more usual to see a man taking a dress off a woman than putting it on her but really, it is not that much different is it?" i
"True, sorry about your cardigan" Zelda
"I don't suppose cardigans were designed for such ex- otic use but they did the job" i
"It was exotic, i never had sex by a real palm tree be- fore" Zelda
"I am grateful for all the goodness you brought to it to- night, with such demonstration it can only come back to life" i
"My pleasure" Zelda
"Mine too" i
"I think i should go back to the party, are you coming down too?" Zelda
"I don't feel like i should, i think i should remain on the happy ending" i
"You're right, it's nice like that" Zelda

She rearranges her hair, taking away the signs of the

wilderness we've been through. I open the door and let her lead the way inside through the narrow space between the bedrooms. We lower our voices, the communal space is all empty and dark.

"Cute bedroom" Zelda
"A bit small but i like it" i
"The staircase is quite steep though" Zelda
"Yeah careful, maybe let me go down first, so i can hold you if you want" i
"No don't worry, it's fine, you stay here" Zelda
"I'm gonna walk you to the door at least" i
"No, no, your bedroom is just here, you just stay here" Zelda
"But the front door can be a bit difficult sometimes" i
"I'm sure i can work out how to open a door on my own, you stay there" Zelda
"Seriously, the front door can be confusing" i
"You, stay, here" Zelda
"You sure?" i
"Pretty sure" Zelda
"But it is not really in the codes of politeness, not to walk a woman to the door" i
"Sometimes politeness can get in the way of simplicity" Zelda
"Certes" i
"Alright, good night" Zelda
"Good night" i
"Bon nuit" Zelda
"Ah oui, bonne nuit" i

I watch her go down the staircase and wait until she disappears under the bedroom, we wave fingers as goodbyes and tell each other the same with the eyes. I close my bedroom door, step out of my moccasins and crawl into bed, post-treatment rest.

Lying on my back, i take a deep breath, spreading my limbs, allowing my spine to relax. I feel relieved and contented, like a hero at the last page of a book. London can count one more happy person, maybe two. I am thinking of what i said to Zelda just before the kiss, smiling.

Sometimes you don't need a plan, you just need a plant, and a meteoroid that has been travelling for millions of years to enter the atmosphere, lighting up the sky and lighting the way at the right moment.

[Vlam!]

by Alain Brémond-Torrent

Bookdesign
Fabian Min-Ho Segginger

Special Thanks to
Mathieu Cuenant,
Donal Sweeney and
Jessica Brown
who helped me make this book.

Printed in Great Britain
by Amazon